Heart
Like A
Truck

Ali Marie

Heart like a Truck
By Ali Marie

©Copyright 2022 Ali Marie
Names, Characters, and events are fictitious, unless otherwise stated. Any resemblance to real person, living, dead, or actual event is purely coincidental. All rights reserved, no part of this book may be reproduced, distributed, or transmitted in any form or by means without the prior permission of the author.
Book Design by Cover Me Softly

Dedication:

To my girls. Christin, Erica and Jamie. The adventures we go on, the moments that find us and the memories we make will last a lifetime. Thank you for always being there through all the tears, crazy ass moments and for filling the space with laughter. For always being my number one fans screaming the loudest.

Preface:

Content Warning: Though this is a romance novel, it does contain triggering situations where characters are involved in violence, physical and verbal abuse, graphic language, PTSD, and mentions of rape along with other explicit sexual situations for 18+.

PlayList:

Southside Of Heaven - Ryan Bingham

Rodeo - Garth Brooks

Hallelujah - Ryan Bingham

She's like Texas - Josh Abbott Band

I Make Myself - Lainey Wilson

The Cowboy Rides Away - George Strait

Heart Like A Truck - Lainey Wilson

Cowgirls Don't Cry - Ronnie Dunn & Lainey Wilson

How 'bout them Cowgirls - George Strait

Tougher - Lainey Wilson

DreamCatcher - Lainey Wilson

Gravel - Lainey Wilson

Better Together - Luke Combs

PROLOGUE: NASH

Three days before…..

We are in a dimly lit spare bedroom of my penthouse because the thought of sharing my personal bedroom with a one night stand is unfathomable. This is all it is, one woman for a good time for one night.

Typically I would opt for a hotel room, but tonight we seem to be closer to home. All thanks to Blake's wild hair for going out on a Wednesday night to let loose a little from an already stressful week.

Now I have a gorgeous blonde in my arms with voluptuous breasts that I have spent several minutes suckling on and a hell of an ass. Believing her name is Alex, I toss her onto the bed in just her laced black knee-high stockings clipped to her matching panties and a barely covering her tits bra. She curls her finger to come to her, informing me she must not truly know who I am. I am the man that will give you pleasure you never knew you needed or wanted. The pleasure only one can dream of. I am the man that says when and how. All with no questions or attachment. Pulling her by the legs, I flip her over.

"On your knees. Ass out." She obeys but not without pouty lips and a flicker of thought to argue.

"You must not have paid too close to the rumors before approaching me. Or you would know not to pout those sweet lips at me," I whisper, learning down near her ear while dragging my finger down the side of the garter. POP! She yelps, eyes going wide.

"What is your safe word, Alex?"

Breathlessly, she purrs, "My name is Ana. Safeword is Purple."

"My apologies, Ana. Please remember your safeword. This is for your benefit, not mine. Understood?"

"Y.yyy.esss," she finagles out. I slowly glide her panties and garters off her legs, letting them fall to the ground. With a pinch of my fingers, her bra falls down to the bed where she sits on all fours, breathing heavily, waiting for what's to come. I slap her ass, then rub it. Once she untenses, I slap it again.

"Deep breaths, Ana." Sliding two of my fingers down her backside, I plunge them into her pool of wetness. "See how your body is already responding to my touch." Pulling my fingers in and out of her folds before picking up pace, I push her to want more. Once her pussy tightens and tenses as she approaches the edge, I pull out and flip her over onto her back. She spreads her legs wide, matching the smile on her face. Stepping out of my slacks and boxers, I approach her entrance while I roll on a condom. Teasing her with the tip as I slightly press in, her moan lets me know she needs more. I slam myself inside of her, picking up a punishing pace. Making her grasp the comforter in clenched fists. Ana tightens her legs around my waist, pulling me in deeper. Thrusting harder into her while her cunt squeezes around my cock as she begins to peak again. Moving my hand slowly down her lower abdomen, my thumb presses and circles her clit. This sends her over the edge, screaming. A few more thrusts and my shaft is pulsing release into the condom inside her. I pull out and walk into the bathroom to dispose of it. Walking back in for round two, I hear, "Purple."

"Purple? We were just getting started," I question back.

Blushing, she murmurs, "I am not sure I can take anymore of you. No, wait, I know I cannot take anymore. Don't get me wrong, that was the best sex I have ever had. But you just…. God… I don't even know what to say…. Thank you, I guess." Ana looks up at me with a pleased but confused look on her face.

"Well, I aim to please. Get dressed, and I'll walk you out."

Ten minutes later, Ana is gone, leaving me with an unfulfilled release. She had me thinking she would play the role of submissive. Partake in being tied up and teased. Once I threw her on the bed, I should have just stopped, but something told me she needed a release, and *fuck,* if it hadn't been a week since my last rendeavours. My dick feels underappreciated when actual work calls.

Entering my shower to rinse Ana and her heavy perfume off, I try to think of what latest lay I can jerk myself too. Not many come to mind. The women I have had lately either think they want to partake in my kink of control, of dominance, but few last past the sprinkled vanilla I offer up first. Knowing being a submissive is not for everyone, I do try my damndest to ease them into it. After all, I am a gentleman and have a family name to keep in good standing.

Chapter 1: Break

A pure state of angst is what I am in tonight. We have been planning this night out for the last eight months, even before my life turned a 180 six months ago. A situation where one might say, "when you fall off a horse, you get back on." In the most literal sense as well as in *girl, you need to get your shit together. Life handed you a tough break, but move on at this point.* I am excited to be with my ladies tonight, hanging out at the stock live show and concert tonight because my man Ryan Bingham is performing. Essential urban country artist that wrenches one's soul with his songs. Not to mention that whiskey voice and rustic rough look of a cowboy. Other than that excitement; I am most definitely sick to my stomach because the last time I was there, my whole life trajectory changed.

I knew I should not have pushed Doc Holiday as hard as I did, being that he was only coming off a sprained ankle that was cleared three weeks prior by my vet. Hell, who am I kidding, that horse of mine is more competitive than any human I know in this sport. He loves nothing more than to high-tail out through the arena, rounding those barrels at the speed of lighting and taking home the win for all the extra attention. For the last four years, that is exactly what he has done. What we have done. This time felt no different until it all changed. Him and I were coming around the last third barrel of our second run of the day, giving it our all, when I heard it before I even felt what came after. What came after was Doc falling to his left side, landing on my leg and crushing it underneath him, but not before the barrel met the side of my head before going down. It all transpired so fast. I still can't believe it happened the way it did when I re-watch the video.

    Luckily for Doc and me, it was a clean break in his leg, so after surgery that cost me all my savings, he is still around. He may never compete in barrel racing again, but he is such a lovely companion that I am not ready to part with. I also figure he will be my new lesson horse around the ranch. For me, I am told how lucky I am that it was not worse, and that I am able to walk as well as I do. My boot protected my foot pretty well, but I was left with a hip fracture from the fall, heavy bruising all the way down my left leg with a break in my fibula. So after my surgery that I am still paying for, money has been tight. My parents have tried to help, but they are blue-collar workers just trying to stay afloat in this economy and run a dude ranch. My mama is also an English teacher where I also work, so my pa handles most of the ranch work himself along with my older brother. Dirks.

    Also, let me include that my now ex-boyfriend could not handle the pressure of being by my side with having his own rodeo life to live. He took off after a month. Leaving me to deal with rent and bills on my own. Last I heard, he was screwing some buckle bunny from Reno. One of the sexiest cowboys around these parts, so I guess I was blessed that he took me to his bed for the last year. *Insert eyeroll here.* At least that is what his classy self told me before he walked out on me.

    "Now, Willa, you will always be my "first" second love to my ol'girl Dolly out there, but we should have known our time was goin' to run out. Maybe this accident of yours was a blessin' because now we can both walk away guilt free. Okay…. bad choice of words, since you are not walkin', but you know what I mean. Shit, my Willa-bee. This is hard. But you also should know you were the only girl I *shared my bed with over our time together, so that should count for somethin'...... Alright, well I need to be goin', as we head up to Houston for the next leg of the tour. Goin' to miss you not bein' there and doin' your thing and showin' you off. But hey, I'll keep in touch. Bye, Willa."*

With a kiss on the cheek, Luke was gone. Gone with any sense of security I thought I had, my new horse trailer and at the time, I thought my heart. Now my heart just has a few more dents and still pretty pissed about my horse trailer. So needless to say, heading back to the scene of the accident already has my pulse racing and making me pre-game drink.

"Wil! Did you save any shots for any of us?" Tilly shouts at me as she barges into my small cabin, seeing the bottle of whiskey half-empty.

Placing another bottle on the counter, I grin. "Yep, saved a whole bottle for y'all to share."

Tilly has been my best friend since the age of four, when I kicked some little boy's ass for putting mud in her hair. That little boy has grown up to be even more of a pain in my ass then I could have ever imagined. Lana and Amity have been our sidekicks since high school. Tilly and I went to UT on rodeo scholarships, where Amity went to OSU on her scholarship, and Lana completely surprised all of us by deciding not to go to college at all, but became a vet tech. She is probably the one that has the most control of her life at the moment and is engaged to a great guy she met out in Seguin. Tilly graduated with her marketing degree and now works for her dad's marketing firm as one of the managers and barely dabbles in rodeo unless she is helping me. Amity got her degree in agriculture, and after helping with her parents ranch for a year, she somehow found her way to becoming an AG professor at the local community college.

    Me on the other hand; I received my degree in sports management, and now I am the physical education teacher at my local high school and assistant coach to my old rodeo coach, Coach Meader. All this, while still competing on the weekends for the rodeo grand championship. Well at least up until six months ago. Since everything transpired six months ago, I have not even ridden a horse. With my luck, the accident happened right when school was starting back. So I was pretty banged up and healing when school started back, but Coach Meader has been a doll about me coaching from the sidelines and not from a horse. This is where I need to get my *shit together.*

Coach needs me on my horse, on any horse to help train. Our ladies have a complete lack of luster without me showing them out. They need it to be pushed, to train from the best and ride with the best. That is supposed to be me. Me to help them uphold the state championship title in barrel racing, cutting, pole bending, and team roping. The high school hasn't won a National title in any of those since Tilly and I, and that was three years in a row. Now it has been seven years, and the title is long overdue.

I hear, "1, 2, 3, shot!" That pulls me from my thoughts. Only to look over to see my three ride and dies playing a drinking game. I join for a few rounds, enough to make me feel even more tipsy. Hence why we have an uber on its way. The first night in a long time, I am letting loose and going to enjoy myself as much as it may kill my liver. There is always tomorrow, and if my hangover is not beating me down, I can try to get back up on that horse.

CHAPTER 2: OYSTERS

"Hell, that guy is relentless! Nash, did you see that? Sinclair was refusing to be bucked off before eight seconds. He should get extra points for being able to stay on that huge motherfucker as gracefully as he did," Blake, my youngest brother, shouts back at me. It is guys night out and one of the biggest nights of the year around here. So we have taken full advantage of our family suite for the evening, as we make sure to every year. Us brothers and a few of our good friends. One of the few nights we choose not to involve our investors when trying to wine and dine them. This is our night to enjoy. No work, no women, no real world consequences.

    We have the finest food and drinks being poured with the greatest company I know to keep. Including my best man, Fletcher, who goes everywhere I go. He is my golden sidekick as much as the two-legged ones that seem to press themselves within my life. Several events in and it's been a crazy evening with some of the biggest ball buster bulls we have seen to date. Even the broncs have been on the edge between crazy and deranged. Not one man has met eight seconds tonight.

    I would say it is usually pretty calm up in the suites, as where it opens up, you can typically see those near you in the adjoining suite balconies. The party crowd typically hangs out on the floor and lower levels. Those are the ones I see the rodeo clowns have the most fun with along with the jumbotron out to embarrass whoever they can capture in the moment. Like I said, typically it's calmer and slightly classier up here, minus several suites down; I can hear shouts and explicits even all the way over in our suite. It must be a bachelorette party of *many* women because though I am unable to see them well enough, they sure as hell are loud enough for all the suites up here in this row combined. Hours have gone by, and they are still going strong.

    The guys keep joking about going over and telling them to calm their asses down, or screw a few of them in the bathroom to see if that will shut them up. Look, we are men, but gentlemen. What we say behind closed doors, does not represent how we would actually handle a situation. Me, I am just going to keep sitting here, sipping my scotch and enjoying the show. The concert is about to start, and we are in for a treat with Ryan Bingham tonight. That is one thing I am sure of at this moment, as I prop my boots up on the seat in front of me.

    All the sudden our suite door swings open with a very loud voice of "Tilly! You won't bel…."

    Before this bewitchingly, straight-haired fiery red beauty realized she just flew into the wrong suite, she was ready to say something. Now she makes eye contact with all these men standing in attention including my cock and staring in her direction. Her ice blue eyes take a gander around the room when they land and lock on me. Time stands still between us. My jaw begins to pulse as I take in her insatiable lips and body. Our eyes lock with a blaze of want. Or so I thought.

    With a simple wiggle of her nose, then a breath in, she squeals,"O my Hades….. I am going to be sick." Her hand flies over her mouth as she is unsure where or what to do next. I see her eye the trash can across the room, but before I can even move to get it, the girl has found the buffet server of fried oysters. Though it is the most calm and quiet mess I have ever witnessed, she is definitely puking in the oyster tray. We all just stand there gawking. We have all seen our fair share of some gross crazy shit, but this is on a whole other level of our adult lives. As this scene plays out in front of us, we hear another lady walk by, hollering the name of Willa.

Clint takes a chance, "In here!" he shouts. The lady turns to us and steps inside the suite. With one look, she chuckles, "Yep, that's my girl." She walks over and addresses the situation, then bellies over in laughter. This girl is striking too, in her cowgirl getup, blonde wavy hair and petite body, but for me, nothing compares to this redhead that just beguiled my mind and body. Even if she vomits all over our food in front of us. After a few seconds, I finally come back to *planet now*, moving my feet to grab her some napkins, while her friend is basically on the floor rolling with laughter. As I reach this person, I believe now to be Willa, I hand her the napkins. Just as I am about to speak up, she quickly grabs them, then turns her back to me. I can tell she is trying to clean herself up. Once she turns back around, she looks completely mortified.

"Are you okay?" I ask. The need to protect her from maybe even herself is fueling through me.

"No...no I do not think I am. I promise you I am not usually like this, but drinking that much and then the smell of those things," as she points to what once was delicious fried oysters, "it just did me in. Wow. I am a classy broad for sure tonight." Letting out a moan of angst that makes my dick twitch, she continues, "For the love of all things holy.... I am so ridiculously sorry for puking in your food, for barging into your suite to begin with and now for my friend who cannot seem to get her own shit together....This is beyond fuckstrating."

"It is fine." Is all I can manage to say as I try not to laugh at her words and situation. She must think I am a solemn man of few words because all I can do is stare at her and take in every inch of her features. Willa is curvy in all the right places with hand size breasts, no correction, perfect for my large hands to squeeze, and that is exactly what I want to do. Her deep-red fiery hair falls just below her breast line, which only makes me picture her with no clothes on with the teased look of her hair covering those said breasts with fuck-me eyes and mouth. An ass that I just want to sink my teeth in, while I place my hands on those curvy hips and pull her close to me. I grind my teeth as I find myself jealous of that pair of jeans she is wearing that hugs her lower half so well. I can tell straight away she is not a rich, fake beauty type, but my kind of perfect girl next door beauty with her symmetrical face, *real* refined nose, luscious pink lips, and full cheeks. Her at least five foot and some inches stature has her head perfectly at my chest.

Blake's voice interrupts my thoughts, "No, please, you do not need to pay us for the food."

"No, really I must." I notice her start digging in what I deem is a cross-body fanny pack to pull out cash. *What the hell even is that?* "Look, this is what I have on me, please take it. It's eighty bucks." As she tries to hand it to me, I throw my hands up like the rest of us, to let her know we are not taking it. She looks defeated, telling her friend to get up, as they are leaving. Right before she walks out with her friend, she throws the money on the counter and shuts the door behind them. "Bro, what the fuck was that?" our buddy Alex says. I feel like I am frozen in place, but I hear the muffled sounds of them behind me, joking and discussing what just took place.

"Clint, please go find out who that was and what suite they are in?"

"On it, sir," he says as he salutes me like a smartass and heads out. The rest of the guys finally calm back down, just as Ryan comes on stage for his introduction. Me on the other hand, trying to stoke the fire that was just lit throughout my entire body. Even Fletcher is pawing at my leg as if worried something is about to go down. I take a seat next to Blake to try to focus on the show to calm down along with this raging hard-on in my pants.

~~~

Tilly and I make it back to our suite with the unfortunate event that I have more than sobered up in the last ten minutes then I planned on feeling tonight. Who the fuck was that guy, and what in the underworld was that? I felt the pull to him the instant I walked into the suite. When our eyes locked, my nerves fizzled throughout my body, sending my mind in a million directions. Which in turn led to the embarrassing puking all over their food. Seriously though, who in their right sense eats oysters, let alone enjoys the smell of them fried? Ugh, just the thought has my mouth watering with bile again.

The scent of bourbon feels my nose, bringing me to the present.

"No water?" I grimace, taking the glass from Amity's hand.

"Nope. Best way to cure the thought of vomiting again is to keep drinking."

"Not sure that is correct, but hades, cheers to not puking again."

"Cheers!" my girls shout after me.

The bourbon quenches the thirst in my throat, but not the one that is burning lower within. A burn of want and need from that honey swirly-eyed man. His eyes haunt my thoughts as I listen to Bingham singing of being lost, of heartache that only a lost soul can feel in the deep parts of their heart. Me, I am that lost soul, holding on to a tattered string, warning it might snap with the lightest breeze.

Tilly is still filling in the girls on the events several doors down, with them trying to guess who those guys were. I wonder to myself who they are. Who he is, because it was like his body and mind were summoning me to him. Maybe even before I stepped foot in that suite.

CHAPTER 3: BEWITCHED

It is almost the end of the concert when I decide to walk down to their suite. Clint had let me know they are three doors down from us, and there are only four of them. No party, just a girl's night out that had been a long time coming. He apparently met one of the other girlfriends named Lana. Just so happens, she is the only one engaged, and word has it, the other three are as single as they can get at the moment. Clint quickly joked with me that he heard redheads were crazy so he will not be touching that one, but he might be all about that petite blonde that was in here earlier. Blake and Alex are already fighting over the fourth girl, when they have no clue who she is or what she looks like. Luckily the ladies do not have to fear for the others, as they are engaged or already married. Willa definitely needs to fear me.

Fletcher follows me down as I prepare, trying to get my nerves under control to knock on the door. Before I can even knock, the door swings open, and a body slams on to mine. Looking down, it is not just any body, but my bewitching redhead.

"Shit!" she hisses as she steps back to take me in. This time instead of her eyes locking on mine, I can feel her eyes steadily fixate over me. From my boots, up my body very slowly before she gets to my face and finally meets my eyes. I notice her ice blue eyes have more of a glint to them now, and I again find myself lost for words against her alluring beauty.

I hear a sigh, then she utters, "Look, man, I am not sure how much more I can apologize. Trust me, I am completely embarrassed and ashamed of myself that I do not need a lecture from the likes of you. Is it more money? Do I need to grovel?"

My hand quickly goes up in front of her face to tell her to be quiet. She looks pissed, but she snaps her mouth shut. *Damn, she is a fiesty one, but hell if my cock did not miss the second she became submissive. Good girl.*

"No, not at all. I am not here for any of that. I actually came down here to give you your money back because I would not be much of a gentleman if I were to keep it, now would I?" She rolls her eyes at me then looks back to her friends, who are schemingly grinning. My palm twitches to want to spank her for the attitude.

"Please take this back. Really," I murmur as I extend my arm to hand her money back.

"Fine, if you insist." She reaches to take it, and her finger tips touch my hand, lighting another fire within. I notice a slight pause in her movement as well, before she moves her hand and puts the money back in what I now deem as a fanny pack.

Ruff, Ruff.

We both look down together at Fletcher.

"Um, did Lassie follow you from home?" she quickly asks.

"Something like that. This is Fletcher, and he goes everywhere I go."

"Oh. So like a support service dog?"

"Something like that."

"Something like that, got it," She says it back with another eye roll. *Jesus, she is making it hard to not punish her in the most pleasurable way.*

Clearing my throat, I ask, "Look, can we start over? My name is Nash." I reach out again, this time putting my hand out for her to shake. Without even hesitating, she places her hand in mine.

"I'm Willa. These are my ride and die, Tilly, Lana, and Amity."

I notice the guys about to walk up. "Can we please walk you down to your car?"

The one I now know as Tilly speaks up, "We are taking an uber back, so no need to wait in that chaos unless you already are."

"Nah, I just called our driver. He will be at the curb in ten," Clint speaks up, sending a wink back to her.

Feeling like I am going to lose this battle, I look back at Willa. "Please. I would feel better if I stayed while you waited. A bunch of lovely ladies should not be hanging out there with all the drunken men this late. Besides, I would totally offer to take you back myself, but the car is already full with all of us."

The dark haired girl named Amity speaks up this time. Her voice is sultry and harsh, "These boys must really not know who they are messing with." The ladies start to simper with each other.

Clint laughs under his breath, "This is great because they don't know who we are either." All I can do is punch him in the shoulder to shut up.

Finally Willa takes another gander at me then speaks back up, "Sure, you can walk us down."

Trying to keep my christmas grin underwraps, I nod and wait for the ladies to pass by Willa and me. I place my hand on the small of her back, against her soft velvet skin that her crop top does not cover as we walk down and out of the arena. Once outside, I can tell it has started to get chilly this February evening. Without asking, I take my suit jacket off, placing the jacket around her shoulders. Barely meeting my eyes, I hear a whispered, "thank you" from her. We get to where the lanes split off between those leaving from on one side of the lot, to the rideshares on the other. The guys go with Clint to get in our car, and we just give a knowing nod.

To my brothers and friends, they probably cannot remember the last time they saw me with a woman I was interested in for more than sex. Let alone held any interest since my highschool sweetheart Melanie. That was about nine years ago and not one until now has piqued my interest to have a conversation with and not just a good time. They know I am not leaving here until I have this woman's number.

We make small talk about the rodeo and concert highlights while we wait. Finding out she is a huge Bingham fan herself, even before he became famous for that show Yellowstone. Tilly had informed the group their uber driver is thirty minutes out. So I am taking this prime time to feel Willa out on who she is. I soon notice a couple up against the fence, just making-out like their drunken-selves depended on it. Willa sees me shaking my head, sniggering and staring, so she turns around and proceeds to watch the same drunk shit show I am. The man's hands are above his head locked into the fence, as the woman's fingers are linked through the fence behind the guy's back. I honestly do not think either one of them has come up for air in the few minutes we have been staring.

Shaking her head, she turns back to me and murmurs, "Some people just can't make it back to their hotel rooms, I guess." Laughing out loud, I pull my phone out to video tape this.
"Hey, act like I am video-ing you, but I am going to capture this for Clint. He will get a kick out of it." She nods, and I push play. As I have them in the background, my main focus becomes Willa. She is taking her job very seriously, as she continues to make faces at the camera and does a turn. At one point she scrunches up her nose and makes the cutest face followed by her blowing a kiss at me. Again, I am just in awe of her beauty and her presence, and Clint will no longer be seeing this video.

Then a large group of people walk by with a guy who shouts out, "Damn, I wish that was me right now!" He points to the fence couple, causing everyone nearby to laugh, along with me wishing that was me with Willa up against me. *Maybe even have her arms tied to the fence holes so there is no way she can touch me. Only allowing me to tease and pleasure her.* Putting my phone back up, I walk up to her with ease and rub my hands up and down her arms like it is the most natural thing for me to do. She doesn't even flinch but steps in closer to my body for some more warmth. Electricity of familiarity shoots through me, making the hair on my arms standup. No way she does not feel this same current.

Bringing us out of our little box, she quickly turns around when we hear, "OOOO weee. Look here boys on who I just found. Our favorite buckle bunnies."

"Son of a bitch," she whispers while looking back at her friends, then to the guys standing next to us. "Fuck off, Tucker. You cannot still be mad for Tilly and I beating you at ropin'. Besides, the difference between us and your buckle bunnies is that we can actually ride more than just a cock."

I hear the crowds start ooo-ing, and the girls come together like they are about murder someone. My eyes grow wide as I try to address the situation playing out in front of me. Willa turns to look back at me as if warning me not to engage in this.

"Oh, sweetheart, it's just because you haven't let mine break you in yet. Must be why you keep showing up everywhere I am," this asshole spews out, while I am trying hard not to jump over these girls and kick his ass myself. I see my brothers and friends walking towards me, sensing they must have gotten nosy when they saw the crowd start to circle up.

"Go walk in hell. Besides I have more buckles than you and your crew combined, so who is following who again?" Willa speaks up, and I can tell her cheeks are a fire red, not because she is cold, but because she is pissed.

"Really there, sweetheart? When was the last time you got on that broken horse of yours or any horse at all and took a title home?"

Willa lunges for him, and as her girlfriends have her complete back and about to jump in with her, I am quick to wrap my arm around her waist and pull her back and step in front. "The lady said fuck off, so you need to respect that and leave." My guys are now behind me, waiting for a good fight.

"Well, what do we have here? Looks like our Willa found herself a new toy!...Hey man, I hear she likes it rough."

With that, my clenched fist meets his jaw, and he goes down fast and hard. I remain posed and unphased at this point, but I am ready to kill this guy if he speaks one more word. Tucker's friends soon gather around him, and I see one whisper something in his ear, causing him to look up at me, to the guys around me, and back at Willa.

Slowly standing up with what seems the realization of who I am, he chokes out, "Not looking for a fight man. Sorry. Just messing with my girl and her group. No harm, man." As soon as the last words leave his lips, they all quickly scatter away.

"What the hell is going on tonight?" Alex asks. The rest of us shrug our shoulders as the crowd disperses.

"Ten minutes," Tilly says nonchalantly about their driver, like I did not just punch a guy nor that they were fired up enough to do some massive harm to those guys.

Willa turns back around to me and nibbles her lower lip. "Um, not sure what just happened, but thank you, even though you didn't have too. Thank you. And let me profusely apologize on behalf of those assholes. They are just a bunch of shitin' cock-wad nobodies."

"Cock-wad. Going to have to add that one to my vocabulary, along with fuckstrating." This makes her laugh, and god, it is a heart-skipping pleasing sound.

"There is a lot to unpack in what just transpired here in the last several minutes, but I'm going to save that for another conversation." Handing her my phone, I ask, "Can I please have your number?"

"Very forward, but I like that." She takes my phone and starts inputting her number then lets out a little giggle to herself.

"What did you just do?" My brows scrunch as she hands my phone back to me.

"I won't divulge what I thought of doing, but time will tell on me for what I actually did."

"I look forward to punishing you then." My voice comes out deep and husky as I give Willa a wink and move on, but keep my eyes on her, waiting as she processes what I just said. My lips tip up in a grin as her eyes go wide with curiosity more than fear.

Looking at my phone, I see nothing un-ordinary. So I hit *call,* causing her phone to ring. She looks at it and then back at me. "There, now you have my number and know it's me when I contact you." I see her smile while programming my number.

"Hey there, hot stuff, I need to steal my girl away because our ride is here."

"Not a problem." I lean down and place a kiss on her cheek, with my hand on her arm, whispering in her ear, "Until next time." I can feel the shiver that runs down her body as she turns and looks at me. Mouths merely inches away before she is pulled away from me and pushed inside the blue Tesla that quickly drives off.

Chapter 4: Speed

    Our Uber driver, Jake, is the coolest we ever had. None of us small town ladies have been in such a neat car, so he was more than happy to oblige us by stepping on the gas pedal at the redlight, surging the car to sixty mph in under six seconds then floored to one hundred mph. It seems so effortless for this car to do, unlike my Chevy pickup truck that begins to shake at seventy. He even opens the huge moon roof for us to gawk at and shows us a few other nifty Tesla kinks for the car. Best part is, he even gets out when he reaches my place to take a picture of us in front of the car and then takes a selfie with all of us. Really a cool way to end the night. We were having too much, that I didn't even have time to process my time with Nash.
We walk in my cabin, and as I go to check the time on my phone, I see I already have a text from Nash. Who is this tall, dark featured, lean but fit, whiskey eyed, presiding of a gorgeous man? I swear it's as if he fell out of the sky because I have never seen him

around, but felt frighteningly connected to him. It makes sense I guess that I have not seen him before because he clearly reeks of prestige and money. Far cry from this side of the barn. Looking back down at my phone, I smile.

Nash: Please let me know you got home safely.
Me: Just walked in my door. We had a wild ride in the Tesla going 100mph down the back road to my house.
Nash: That does not seem safe. Should you report him?
Me: Oh my Hades, NO! We asked him too. He was kinda outnumbered.
Nash: Wow, okay. You like speed...taking notes.
Me: Curious to know what other notes you have on me.
Nash: Too many pages to go through this late.
Me: HAHAHA... oh my. Did you and the guys all make it home okay? And I also have your jacket.
Nash: Yes, thank you for asking. Everyone is at their places, except Blake is staying with me tonight since we have a work engagement tomorrow over in Victoria.
Nash: Just keep it. I have several.
Me: Like a souvenir? Thanks. Sunday work. That is no fun.
Nash: Nothing new here for me. Any plans?
Me: Other than recovering from the hangover I am going to have, not too much. Just helping my parents around the ranch and maybe some riding.
Nash: Good luck with that. My thoughts and prayers will be with you.
Me: Thanks, they will be put to good use, smartass.

Nash: Just trying to be a gentleman. ……. Are you free to facetime?
Me: I am. Let me sneak out of my house the girls are starting to pour shots again.

Ring…Ring…..

"Hey…. Can you see me good enough? I am out under the porch light on the swing."

"Yes, I can see your alluring self."

"Don't make me blush, sir. It has already been a long night and an embarrassing one."

"Willa, please do not sir me, unless you want me to give you a reason."

This man is going to be the death of me if he keeps saying off kiltered words like that with his sinister smolder. It is like he stepped out of one of my romance novels I keep hidden behind all my non smut books on my shelves. Living in a cabin on your family's dude ranch means not much privacy. I have caught my mama plenty of times in my house, whether she is leaving me a meal, some mail or what not, and I know she has circled the rooms around snooping. I think it becomes part of a parent's DNA once they have children.

I take in Nash's background on the screen. He is sitting on a couch, but I can see the walls behind him are shiplapped, and there is a huge stone fireplace in the corner of the room. Based on how he was dressed tonight, the fancy Cadillac SUV they rolled out in and now this, he is most definitely out of my league.

"Yes, Sir," flies out of my mouth with a smile and wink. Which then he nods his head as if he is mentally taking more notes on me. "So, who are you?" I break the silence of staring at his clenched jaw. "Tonight you and your group were all dressed in your swanky suits, high priced cowboy boots, and hats, but I am not buying you to be the true cowboy type."

He lets out a huff of a laugh. "Cowboy type, huh? Let us see... I can ride a horse western or bareback and have participated in several cattle drives and still do when I can. I always wear my cowboy boots unless I am exercising, partaking in a water activity, or carnal activities. I drive a pick-up truck."

"Hold your horses there, cowboy. I will come back to carnal activities, but first what type of truck?"

"Why do I get the feeling this is going to make or break me?" All I can do is shrug my shoulders and grin. "It is a super duty F-250 King Ranch." I start laughing because it's as if he is holding his breath waiting for my reaction.

"Nope, I cannot date a Ford guy. Sorry."

"Are you serious right now?" He gives me a face that reminds me of my brother when his dog was hit by a car. I mean he lived, but it was the saddest look I'd even seen. I had noticed Nash's dark brown eyes with a light honey swirl in them that was hypnotic from earlier. Now they look a little dimmer.

"Oh my goodness, you took that to heart, real quick.... It's fine. A few points deducted from your status, but it's fine. Being a Chevy girl, it is the King Ranch edition that is saving your ass right now. I can't go against the King Ranch being that it is a staple in our state, and I know several ranch hands down there." Finally looking like he can breathe again, I change the subject. "I am interested in hearing about these cattle drives, but we can save that for another time. I know it is late, and it sounds like you have a busy day tomorrow."

"I am fine staying on the phone with you. I am enjoying this conversation too much and enjoy watching the light hit the side of your face perfectly as you swing. Even keep catching a few glimpses of stars behind you."

"I can hang for a bit longer. It sounds like the girls have finally wind down. But yeah, it is beautiful out here with all the open space and sky. You must be in the city if you appreciate my scenery."

"That I do. I have a house out in Horseshoe Bay, but most of my time is spent at my apartment in the heart of SA. That is where I am now. Too many city lights to really see the sky."

"Wow, Horseshoe Bay….and from the looks of it, your apartment living room is bigger than my whole cabin."

"Well, that's just thanks to a long standing family business that has been successful enough to be passed off to me to r... to work at."

"Okay, so I take it you are a family man?" I am trying to keep my cool, as this man apparently has more money and luxuries than I could have dreamt up.

"Yes. You met my brothers tonight. We all work for the family business. Each of us handles different aspects of the firm. My dad still likes to help drive decisions and be part of it all, but now he spends most of his time at my mother's side, traveling. I am not sure that man will truly ever retire. But yes, when they are home, we have family

Sunday dinners and a few vacations a year we all spend together. They are good wholesome people."

Speechless over here, and I have even stopped swinging. "Can I get your last name, Nash?"

"Would you be offended if I told you I do not want to divulge that information until after our first date?"

"No, not offended, just making me more curious."

"Well, how about I take you out for a date next Saturday? I would prefer sooner, but I know what my calendar already consists of for the week."

"Um…. sure."

"I can pick you up, and we can head out to dinner and see where the night takes us."

"I am more than happy to meet you in the city if that is easier. I do live off the beaten path."

"Not a problem, and that means I just get more time with you."

"Smooth talker…. I'm starting to take notes." He just laughs, and it's deep and endearing.

"Alright then, I am going to let you go so you can get your rest, but text me your address. Can I call you sometime tomorrow?"

Smiling, I murmur, "Um, okay. That sounds good… Good Night, Nash."

"Good Night, Willa."

After hanging up, I quickly shot off the address to the Crenshaw's Hey Dude Ranch, figuring he can meet me over at the main house, since it's a lot nicer than my little wooden cabin. Setting my phone on the counter, I see Lana and Amity are passed out on the sofa bed. I head to my room and crawl into bed with Tilly, who is drunk-out with her eye mask on. Visions of Nash dance through my head, and for the life of me, I cannot figure out why the likes of him would want anything to do with me.

~~~

It is two in the morning, and I still have not been able to fall asleep. One, I cannot get my mind off the entirety of Willa. Her voice, her laugh, her body in those Wranglers and crop top she wore, with her red hair waving down her back, and those ice blue eyes that memorize me. The familiarity of belonging. How I want to tie her to my bed, lick her inch for inch, making her beg for me to plunge into her. Second, as soon as she sent the name and address of the ranch, my mind raced with the name Crenshaw and why it sounds so damn familiar. *Clint. Clint will know.* Not caring how late it is, because if I know him, he is still up gaming or binge watching some show, I call him.

"Dude, do you know what time it is?" he asks grumply.

"Seriously, you asleep, man?"

"No, I am just messing with you. You are too easy to guilt."

"Fuck, it's been a long of enough night already."

"Woman problems already, brother?"

"Well not until the last thirty minutes, no. I think she is everything I'm not prepared for and more. Which brings me to my question. Does the last name Crenshaw ring a bell?"

"Hmmmm, it does. Let me pull up the files." I hear typing a way and then, "Got it."

"Is this going to be good or bad news for you?"

"Crenshaw is Willa's last name. Her family owns the Crenshaw Dude ranch."

"Well shit. You know how to pick'em. I am not going to sugar coat this for you brother. Our family's company has been after their land for over fifty years. There is sizable evidence the land houses an oil well. Because the property has been in the Crenshaw family for forever it seems and it's owned outright, they have been able to deny us and any other company pushing to drill the land. It was not turned into a Dude Ranch until about forty-five years ago, but it has always housed animals, sanctuary for rescued wild horses and housing. Looking at the company goals for this year, Crenshaw is at the top to convince and conquer. According to Grandfather's notes, these are hard-working people not looking to get rich but to enjoy their lives and what they do. But looks like he was hell bent for years on acquiring this land. I love that this man kept detailed records of his thoughts on business. But Dad thinks the lawyers might have found a loophole to access the well. If I remember correctly, old man Crenshaw used to be force to reckon with, but can't say I expect any difference now from meeting that firecracker related to him. Never met her father."

"Right...... damn, Clint. How the hell are we going to do this?"

"Which deal do you want to walk away from? Your family company that you now run in the name of love or walk away from her before it gets serious?"

I run my hands over my face in disbelief and frustration. The realization sinks in that if she realizes who I am, she will only think I am interested in her family's land. That I concocted this whole plan in some crazy scheme to get close with her.

"I don't know, man. I am supposed to take her out next Saturday evening. I was going to tell her my last name after I charmed her. Now I am thinking it is not such a great idea."

"Which part?" he asks.

"Any of it. I Facetimed her for about an hour tonight on the phone, just getting to know her a little more and filling her out. Willa has my mind and body feeling and thinking things I did not think were even possible anymore. I cannot imagine what more time with her would do to me. There is something about her, Clint. My nerves are shot to hell. Fletcher laid on top of me the whole conversation because he probably thought I was about to have a moment."

"Shit, man, that bad? After a few hours of knowing her?...... Look, I love you and want to see you happy more than anyone. Because you are worthy of happiness despite whatever you think in that thick skull of yours. So you need to be honest with her upfront. Clear the air, so she is aware of who you are, and that you are not one to mix business and pleasure. That what you want with her is separate from what your career is. If she feels that strongly about it, she can ask you to walk away from her or the land. Then you can make a decision." Clint suggests, and I feel like that is so much easier said than done. This relationship is going to be over before it starts.

"Bro, did we know a Willa when we were younger? I can almost remember a red headed freckle face kid hanging around when we were kids."

"You know my memory is shit. Besides, what are the odds?"

"That's true, but I'll look more into it."

"Thanks man. Well I am going to try and get some rest before tomorrow's travel and meeting.

"Keep me posted. Bye."

With that, I find myself tossing and turning with all the inner turmoil until Blake pulls my zombie ass out of bed.

Chapter 5: Huckleberry

I knew I should have locked that damn rooster up yesterday. "It is only 5:30 in the morning" I yell out, startling Tilly awake. She goes from sitting straight up, groaning to falling back on the bed. I go ahead and get up, heading to the kitchen to make some strong coffee. We are all going to need it today.

A knock at the door, has me wondering who in the hell is knocking at my door this early? And it better not be my brother. I have until at least seven to get my ass out there. Wrapping my robe tightly around me, I open the door to be greeted with an older man in a black suit. Looking behind him sits a black Cadillac SUV.

"Miss Willa Crenshaw?"

"Yes, can I help you?"

"Yes, this is for you." He hands me two large bottles of some green substance. "This is from Mister Ho....I mean Mister Nash sent this over for you and your friends. A cup of this, and you will be hangover free. It is a concoction the brothers swear by."

"Oh, well, thank you! I will let him know I received it. Hey....how did you know what cabin I was in?"

"Your mother sent me over here. It seems they were already tending to the cattle and horses this morning."

"Gotcha. Well thank you, kind sir. This will be put to good use. Please let Nash know I appreciate it."

"I will, Miss, and have a good day."

I nod and again in shock. Who sends over hangover juice this early in the morning? *This unknown last name, Nash guy, that's who.*

I wake the girls up, and we head to the counter while I pour glasses for each of us. It smells awful, but I am willing to try anything to not feel this shaky and miserable all day. Count of three, we all throw back and swallow. Followed by explicit gagging and making of disgust faces.

"This better work, or I will kill him," Amity spits out, causing the rest of us to laugh as we head to get ready for the day. Lana has more wedding planning to do, but Amity and Tilly are staying to help check-in the newcomers today. Amity gives the horseback tours on the weekend because it is the only time she has to ride these days. Let alone, she has too much fun playing jokes on guests with her reining horse, Nevada, she boards here. Tilly will typically help me give riding lessons to the kids, and right now, she is my star of the show since I have yet to jump back on that horse.

Heading out the door, I pull my phone out to text Nash:

Me: Thank you for the hangover elixir. So far it has worked wonders.
Nash: You are welcome. It is a secret recipe, but let me know when you need more. I will have it delivered.
Me: You are too kind, sir. (winky face) How did you know I would be up that early?
Nash: Took a wild guess. I told Grant if you did not answer to just leave it on your porch with a note. Glad you were up.
Me: I take it you are traveling?
Nash: Yes, Blake is driving. We are still an hour away.
Me: Okay. Well enjoy your work day. I am going to try and wrangle some horses.
Nash: This I would like to see.
Me: Anytime, cowboy. (kiss emoji)
Oh, no... wrong emoji....unsend, unsend.......
Nash: ...

Those damn three dots keep popping up and then going away, then popping up... I throw my phone across my truck and start it up as Amity and Tilly jump in.

DING! Tilly snatches my phone from the seat and reads it out loud.

Nash: You have no idea how much I want to taste you and feel your lips on me.

"Holy horses.....where was this last night? He seemed so quiet."
"Maybe he is one of those quiet CEO types that is dominant in the bedroom. He definitely put off some type of vibe," Amity says, raising her eyebrows up and down, causing me to blush, thinking of the comments he made when I referred to him as sir last night.

"You read too much about Alpha males." I feel my inner workings yearn for something I have not had in a long time.

"Calling the kettle black this morning?" We all just laugh because it is so the truth.

"What do I say back?"

"You don't. At least not right away," Tilly says.

Amity speaks up, "I got a better idea, let's go see some horses. Especially Doc."

As soon as we drive up to the pasture, and I holler for Doc Holiday, he comes not at his usual canter, he comes as fast as he can. Luckily followed by the three other horses that we need for this morning's lessons.

"Hey there, my prince charming," I coo as I rub his face down before placing the halter on him. "You want to come help some today?" Doc answers with a nudge in the face. We get the other three haltered up, and Tilly and I sit on the tailgate, holding on to their ropes as Amity drives slowly to the stables. Sunrise is gorgeous this morning, and there is still a nice morning dew fog that hasn't completely blown away yet. Once at the stables, we tack the three horses, and I leave Doc in his halter. I have no plans on putting him to work today, but I know he enjoys the change of scenery and extra attention he can get from visitors.

Amity comes up to us, holding out her hand. "Give me your phone." I hand it over with a raised brow. "Okay, lay a kiss on your Huckberry over there, and we'll send a pic to Mister dominant."

"I like where you are going." Smiling, I lean over and onto Doc. "Say cheese, Doc!" And he does as I place a kiss on his left cheek.

"Perfect," I giggle as Amity shows me the picture. It really is too. Doc's smile is the best, but he really does it up for this picture with me kissing him."

**Me: Get in line behind my Huckleberry, cowboy.
(picture attached)**

I am getting the disappearing three dots again.....

Nash: I have never been jealous of a horse before. Thank you for the first.
Me: This is Doc Holiday. The current love of my life. And you are very welcome.
Nash: Another note I am jotting down. Tombstone fan?
Nash: Does Doc Holiday know you have a hot date coming up that you will be leaving him for?
Me: Ssshhhh, we do not speak of such things around him. He can get very jealous. And yes on Tombstone.
Nash: Guess I better give him several reasons to be jealous then. It would only be fair.
Me: (video attached)
Nash: Did your horse really flare his nostrils at me?
Me: He is trained well.
Nash. Unbelievable.
Me: (picture attached)
Nash: Stop making me jealous. He gets your kisses and your hugs? I think you have no room in your life for another.
Me: There is plenty of room...
Me: For the right person.
Nash: Sounds like a challenge, and it has been accepted.
Me: (winky face)
Nash: Would you think less of me if I told you I wish next Saturday was here already because I am really looking forward to our date and seeing you?
Me: No, I would think less of you if you didn't.
Nash: (picture attached)

Me: Damn…. Do you just wake up looking that HOT? Sorry, you just got the braid and no makeup look today. I see you traded in your swanky cowboy get-up for casual. I am diggin' it.
Nash: I do, completely effortless, a complete gift.
Nash: Trust me, I feel the same way looking at you. I appreciate that you don't feel the need to doll up or use a filter. Your beauty is undemanding.
Me: That's me! I am sure I play in the dirt more than most girls you have dated. Or ever dated. One thing you will learn about me real quick, I am tough, dirty, and unapologetic.
Me: Just thought I would throw that out there, in case you want to run. Now is your chance.
Nash: Only running to you, Willa.

Gushing…blushing……is this man real?

Nash: Hate to cut this chat, but we just arrived and have to go schmooze some clients on the golf course. Feel free to text me if you want. I will answer when I can.
Me: (picture attached)
Nash: (hearted image)

    I finally look up to see Amity and Tilly gawking at me. "Did you just send him a selfie from atop of Doc?"
    I look down and realize I am sitting on Doc, bareback. Taking a deep breath in, I calm my nerves. "I am on top of my horse!" I whisper-yell as tears roll down my cheeks. I jumped on up here without

thinking twice, just because I wanted to get this picture for Nash. This is huge as I look at my ladies. They get it and are crying with me. Six months, six fucking months, I have tortured myself about getting on a horse, let alone my Huckleberry—post the accident.

"Wil, you did it. Look at you!" Tilly exclaims. I lay down and wrap my arms around my big boy, and Amity snaps a picture on her phone. "This is a moment worth remembering."

"Yes, yes it is!" I exclaim as I slide down off of Doc. My phone dings with the picture Amity just sent me. I immediately save it as my wallpaper. *I can do this. It is time I do this.* With the horses ready, we head out to the arena.

CHAPTER 6: SWING

We are a few hours into Tee time before I feel my phone buzz in my pocket. Fingers crossed it is her, I pull my phone out of my pocket to check. She has been the pinnacle of my thoughts all morning. The arguments in my head about us working out with my company after her parents' land keeps losing to my heart. The realization that this is not going to be my decision in the end hurts. Then the flashes of her from the last twenty-four hours and the pictures she sent this morning take my breath away.

"You alright there, bud?" I hear.

"I am. Sorry. Did you say something?" Looking over, the group of guys including Blake stare back at me. Blake gives me a shift of his eyes to look down, and as I do, I see Fletcher pulling at my pant leg. His que for me to go to the ground to be level with him so he can lay on top of me before the "moment" gets out of control. I bend down to scratch Fletcher's ears, letting him know I am okay.

"No, I am good. I was just running through some things in my head. So, Eddy, if you were to invest fifty thousand, your turn investment would profit over three million in just the next two years. And that is even if that economy goes to hell. Oil is like alcohol, everyone wants and needs it."

"Amen to that!" He cheers and clinks his beer can with mine. "Let's finish this round and we can sign the paperwork over some food and drinks at the clubhouse."

Blake is usually my deal closer, but I think I just impressed myself. My role is typically the face of the company, the ear to hear the concerns and problem solve.

"Great! Let's do this."

"By the way, Nash, you suck at golf," Eddy laughs out.

"Believe me I know, and today is not my best at all," I laugh back.

Blake comes up and puts his hand on my shoulder and rubs it. "You seem good. If it's the redhead, keep her around."

"That's the plan." I grin as he walks away to get his swing ready. I finally pull my phone out to check, and I feel my heart skip with the site of *Willa* scrolling across the screen.

Willa: What's the difference between a G-spot and a golf ball?
Willa: *A guy will actually search for a golf ball.* **(laughing emoji)**

She is making golf jokes. She has me so damn turned on right now because she has no idea what I want to do to her, and I have a feeling I won't need to search for hers.
Me: Trust me, I do not need to search for yours. I already know I can make you come so hard, spilling onto me.

Willa: (open mouth emoji)
Willa: Did Tilly tell you?

Shit, why would Tilly tell me? Has she, does she? I am not sure how to even ask that question or what to say. Either way, it is hot as fuck.

Me: (shoulder shrug emoji)

Just going to play dumb in this conversation until she frees herself of information.

Willa: Well, while we are on the subject. Other than my ears, that is the only other thing I have pierced. Only one tattoo, which is completely hidden unless I am naked. You have any forbidden treasures?

Fucking Christ. She has her damn clit pierced. Now her cunt is all I can think about, along with where this one tattoo could be on her velvet, perfect, slightly tanned skin. Taking my hat off, I fan my face and push my hair back in sexual frustrartion. "*Think of unhappy thoughts man,*" I grumble to myself as I walk over to pick up my club, since it is now my turn to swing if I can get my hard-on to back down. Blake is laughing because he must have been watching my face during that text exchange, and now I am trying to adjust myself. He salutes me as I get ready to swing, and I lose it. Literally, the club goes flying out of my hands before I even hit the ball. Most embarrassing day as the guys have their fun.

"I am going to sit over here on the golf cart and down some beers to find my ego. You gentlemen keep playing." Pulling my phone back out, I hastily type.

Me: Guess you will have to search me.
Willa: Challenge accepted, cowboy.
Me: Just so you know, because of you, I have completely embarrassed myself at golf today.
Willa: Oh, please do tell.
Me: Maybe once I get my ego in-check.
Willa: It's not the size of your putter that counts, it's how many strokes you take.
Me: I am so pleased you are amused.

Willa: I am and can keep going…. The internet is a splendid thing.
Me: No more dirty distractions from you today. (laughing emoji - wink-y face)
Me: I am going to have to punish you if you keep this up.
… … … …
Willa: (picture attached)

    Okay, maybe I stepped into that. She sent over a picture of her, and I am guessing her Chevrolet truck, covered in mud. It must have been from the summer because she is only wearing a bikini top and short shorts with pink rubber boots on. Her hair is up in a messy bun with a big grin on her face.

Me: I think that is the sexiest thing I have ever seen. I am going to dive in the COLD pond at the 16th hole.
Willa: (winky face)

    The caddies have been driving us around, and when I hear Blake's voice holler over to me, I realize they just finished the 18th hole. *Thank you.*

Me: I will chat with you later, beautiful. Work calls.

~~~

    Blake, myself, and Fletcher are finally heading home after a long day on the course, but we closed the deal with the VonDeps, which is a huge win for the Holdings Oil Company. Fletcher is passed out asleep in the back seat. I am sure he is exhausted over these twenty-four hours of a nerved emotional rollercoaster for the both of us.

"So tell me about this, Willa. Other than just meeting her last night, you seem enamored with her."

"Man, she makes me hotter than a damn fever. I have never once felt this way, even with Melanie. And after the last few years post coming home, I did not think it was in me to really feel anything other than pain and guilt again. She has awoken a fire in me. It is more than just wanting to have sex with her." My brothers and I all have our kinks. Blake more so than anyone, and he *loves* everyone. I never thought I had any until I felt the need for control in all aspects of my life. Women know what they are getting when entering a bedroom with me, and I pleasure them until they can't take any more. My rules are no kissing unless I kiss you, and no touching my upper half. For me, it is a pleasurable fix under my control, my dominance.

"Fiery redheads will do that," he says as he laughs at his own joke, only to side-eye me from the passenger seat. "Seriously though, if she can do that for you, then I am all for you being completely distracted. I am going to continue to enjoy all the people I can before I find *the one,* but for you, it's well past time, brother."

"Thanks, I guess. Well, as much as I want to think this is going to go smoothly, Clint and I found a problem early this morning.... Willa is the daughter of the Crenshaws. As in Crenshaw Hey Dude Ranch."

Even through his sunglasses, I can see his eyes bulge out. "Damn, how in the hell? Who did you piss off so badly in the romance sector of your life?"

Shaking my head, I grimace. "I don't even know. I have a date with her next weekend. I plan on calling Dad afterward to get his take on it."

"Please tell me you are going to be up front and honest with her? This can only end poorly if you don't."

"That is the plan. Just wish me luck."

"Bro, you are going to need all of it."

On that note, I scroll through our messages throughout the day and save her pictures to my phone. After this coming up weekend, they could easily be all that I have left of her.

CHAPTER 7: FLETCHER

     Last night, I had only messaged her good night. From the time Blake dropped me at home and from the lack of sleep from the night before, I hit the bed like a rock, and now it is ten the next morning. Finding Fletcher on top of me and body drenched in sweat, leads me to know that I had a rough night. I am sure it's nightmares from my time overseas. The day too many of my squadron were killed, when too many civilians, including innocent children, were murdered and lined the streets as the smoke cleared.

     How I survived, along with just two of my men, is something I will never understand. I was not the one who had a newborn to go home to or even a spouse. Let alone have anyone outside my immediate family waiting on me. Not saying they were not enough, because they were, they are enough. But to the men and women I lost that day in a secret ops mission, I feel like they had so much more to live for. It took months to physically recover from the shards of metal being removed from my whole right side, which ripped through my muscles, leaving scars all over. I was told I was one of the lucky ones that day, but even now, I do not feel lucky. Never have and not sure I ever will come to terms with being alive.

     For the first few months of being home and staying at my parents house recuperating, I would fly to the ground at the sound of a pan falling or a loud bang. I would try to stay awake at night for the fear of the nightmares that awaited me. I lived in a constant state of panic and stress. Therefore I was gifted my golden retriever, Fletcher from a wounded PTSD Veteran fundraiser in our town, and he has been my trusted companion for the past three years. It took me months to come to terms that I had him as I felt there were others more deserving. He eventually won me over, and I am so thankful for him. Even my worst days are not as horrendous as they once were. I am now able to function in an almost "normal" capacity now, which leads me to this feeling Willa gives me. She makes me feel alive, to want to be alive, to push out of this hell hole I have lived in for years. I just hope my time being with her goes as smoothly as I need it to.

Once I finally make it to the office, I am grateful to see all is fairly calm for a Monday. I ignored all calls this morning, knowing I needed to be in the right headspace to deal with whatever bullshit was going to be thrown my way. Now, sitting at my desk, I pull my cell out and turn it on. Just as all the notifications start to populate, my assistant Judy walks in with a stack of paperwork and her sticky notes of return calls. As soon as I realize there is not one message from Willa, I feel my mood shift instantly, and it seems so does Judy. As she politely sets down her hand full of items on my desk, she smiles and backs out quietly, leaving me to ponder my next step. I did just shoot her over a quick text late last night.

Me: Hi, Beautiful.

Five minutes go by and nothing. I'll take it that she is busy so I decide to go about my day. Two hours later, my phone finally dings with her distinct text tone assigned to her.

Willa: Hey, Cowboy. Just saw this. It has been a crazy morning at work. Just now on a short break.
Willa: Hope you got some rest.
Me: I did. Was even late getting to the office.

Willa: *Hope your boss is cool about that, I know mine is not. I won't even tempt it.*
Me: *He is pretty cool about it.*
Me: *I take it your dad is a hard-ass?*
Willa: *He can be, but no. LOL! The Principal of my school is.*

What? Now I am even more confused, so I decide to facetime her.

"Hey. Nice to see your face there, Cowboy. Digging that five o'clock shadow you have going on."
All I can do is smile, seeing her face light up on the other end. "Adding to my notes." She laughs as I scope her background. I see she is sitting at a desk with a bulletin board behind her, but it is hard to make out the letters.
"I assumed you worked at the ranch, so please enlighten me about your profession, Miss Willa."
"I am a teacher, Sir," she says as she winks and gives me the biggest grin. Every time she says Sir, I just want to spank her and give her every reason to call me sir. As if she has caught on to my thoughts, her smile morphs into a wicked grin. "I am a teacher at the local high school."
Then the realization hits me that she just said she was a teacher, and I can not help but laugh "You are a teacher?" When I notice her facial expression does not change from her glare, I stop and apologize.
"Is that so hard to believe?" she asks
"That was the farthest thing from the list of jobs I had picked out in my head for you."
"Why is that?" I sense she is trying hard not to be offended and hang up. My ass needs to back-track quickly.

"Well, with your beautiful uncanny dictionary of words and brass comments, a teacher was not what I was expecting. Sorry if I offended you, Willa."

"Not offended, I get it. To be fair, I am a physical education teacher and assistant coach of the girls rodeo team. So though my mouth is toned down for my job, I would not say my attitude always is." Both of us are laughing now. "Trust me, I make my English teacher mama very proud."

"I bet you do," I say and smirk.

"She was not the happiest when I graduated top of my class in sports medicine with a minor in English then chose to teach physical education. Every once in a while I will cover for her if she needs to be out."

"Top of your class, huh, What school?"

"UT - hook'em horns!" she yells as she flashes the symbol my way. "You?"

Shaking my head, I grimace, knowing my answer will not bode well. "My degree is for A&M."

She gasps and then says, "Nooooo. Another strike against you, Nash. That's almost a punishable offense."

"I know, I know. To be fair on my end, I did mostly online classes and never partook in a football game or wore the school logo or colors." I see her trying to size me up through the phone.

"Hmmmm, you are an interesting person, Sir."

"I could say the same for you, Miss Willa. You seem to impress me and leave me surprised at every turn. So what, are you on a teacher break right now?"

"Well, good! And yeah, I get fourth period to myself for planning and lunch. Sometimes I will have lunch with my mama, but she is doing some extra credit project with a few of her students. So I am just planning for the next month and looking at the high school rodeo schedule coming up and competition."

"What was so busy about this morning?"

"Oh my Hades. High school boys. First period is weight lifting for the football players. They are typically great about spotting for each other, until I turn my back for a minute and have two kids on either side of the school's prized linebacker, putting more weights on either side of the barbell he was already holding in the air. My panic must have scared them because my linebacker dropped all the weight on his chest, and the other two got caught under the weights as it came down. It was a damn scene from the three stooges. All are fine, just some bruising and had to get a lashing from the football coach because of their stupidity, but whatever. Those damn boys are always playing pranks and causing chaos. All in fun, because they are good kids, but one day, one of them will seriously get hurt because of their actions. At least their quarterback has better sense and avoids their juvenileness."

"Wow, sounds like you have your hands full."

"Oh my goodness, between them and the girl drama, trust me, I know more scoop about students and teachers now than I ever did being a student here. Enough about me, how is your day going?"

"Much better now that I have been talking to you." I can tell she is blushing.

"Do you always look that dapper for work?"

"Are you admiring the view?"

"Damn straight I am. Not every day I get a view like this. Though I would prefer to keep admiring you, unfortunately I do only have five minutes to scarf my turkey sandwich down before my room fills with nosy highschoolers."

"Not a problem, Clint just walked into my office anyway. So I will talk to you later."

"Sounds good, Cowboy." With a wink, she is gone.

Looking over at Clint as he takes a seat across from me, I know what is coming.

"Take it you have not told her yet?"

"Not a conversation I plan to have over the phone."

"Okay, brother. Just tread lightly."

Cock-wad blares out from my phone with a yelling Siri. Over and over again. I rush to turn it off and realize it is an alarm setting. "What the hell?" I whisper. Clint is looking bugged eyed, trying to keep himself composed.

"You have something to explain to me, brother?"

"Shut the fuck up." I glare as I start scrolling back through my phone to pull my alarm app up. "I can't believe she did that."

"Who and what?"

"Willa. When I gave her my phone the other night to put her number in, she started giggling. When she handed me the phone back, nothing looked abnormal. But look! She programmed random alarms to go off and plugged inappropriate words to all of them." Now Clint is laughing so hard and loud it causes Blake to run in and see what all the ruckus is.

"I love this girl already. Please keep her around, and please do not turn those off."

"Clint, what if we were in a meeting right now?"

"Even better. You take this job and life too seriously. Loosen up. For someone that stared death in the face, you came back more bearing," Blake throws in.

Shaking my head in disbelief but laughing on the inside, I grin because she is a clever one. "Got it, brothers," I say back. "Can I help you with something?"

"Yes, on a more serious note, I need you to fly out with me to Alabama with me. Some guys got hurt on the job today."

"Alright, fire up the jet and let's go," I say as I jump up and head out with Fletcher hot on my heels. Blake is left back in my office still sniggering.

Chapter 8: Paramour

Tonight is Thirsty Thursday at Paramour. One of Amity's favorite spots to hang because let's just say this place is where us ladies love to hang, where all people are loved, can turn into a complete rager at any given moment, but swanky enough where the elite want in. Amity is convinced the love of her life will show up here one day because the last thing she wants is a cowboy. As much as she loves that life herself, she has seen what that life has done to her own parents from the travel, the booze, the women, the poor-ness, to where her dad can barely move some days. Let alone, Amity plays for both teams. She is hot enough to have any identity lust over her. So us girls are here to support her, and we always enjoy the company.

I have not heard too much from Nash this week since he let me know he was traveling for work. We play five questions daily through texts just to get to know one another more. I'm still unsure of what that man does, and I refuse to google him in fear of what I might find before he can share himself. Which he promises to do on our date on Saturday. Right now, I can tell you his favorite color is ice blue. His favorite place to visit is Portugal, followed by his nickname in high school was the "Real McCoy" as he was the star quarterback. Favorite food is tacos, and choice drink is scotch. So for a nice distraction, tonight I am letting loose with my ladies because tomorrow is Friday, and it is jeans day. Plus my school has an early release for the basketball championship game that the boys team is playing in.

~~~

    Blake and I find ourselves out at this new club tonight because we have clients in town who requested it. I will be the first to admit I feel slightly out of place as it is not my typical scene. Not because of what it represents, but there is so much going on. Between the drag show downstairs, ladies night, a selfie bar, the drink menu alone has me questioning my choices that got me here. Not to mention, there seems to be a rumored sex corner on top of this rooftop bar. As I eye the area that I see divided off, I can only imagine what is going behind the walls. The clients we are hosting tonight are a bit eccentric and have a very open marriage. All of us brothers have been privy to their flirtatious asks. I am still not sure if Blake has partaken or not because he can be a closed book when he wants, but we all know he has a splendid time with every beautiful person he finds. Plus he knows our rule, we do not mix business with pleasure, with now Willa being that one exception. We are chatting it up as our clients Sarah and Paul keep their eyes out for potential hook-ups, and I am almost convinced they have reached their max on the facial and panty dropper drinks after only an hour.

It finally quiets down a little as it seems they switch over to a DJ as the dance floor opens up. It is at this moment, I hear her laugh. There is no mistake it is Willa. I quickly excuse myself and make my way over to the rooftop bar where I spot the side of her with her friends and several guys, with her hand on one of their shoulders as she laughs. Not that I have any right to be jealous, but I am. I take a few seconds to soak her in, as she is wearing those damn tight ass Wranglers, with her brown and turquoise cowboy boots, topped off with a cream colored crop t-shirt that I can clearly see her black bra through. Her hair is in braids under her hat, all flashed over with her belt buckle. Now I am hard and jealous, fuck. Instead of storming over there, I decide to take my time on getting over there, waiting for the perfect moment to come up behind her.

I whisper in her ear, "Caught red handed cheating already, I see," before placing my hand on her waist.

Without missing a beat, she says, "Yep. You caught me...." and she turns her head my way and winks. Those damn icy blues bewitch me again. "Toby, I would like to introduce you to Nash, the guy I was telling you about. Nash, this is my good friend, Toby, and his fiance, Eric. And this hunk over here is Antony, their out of town lover who is in town for the weekend."

I shake their hands and calm down my jealousy. Well played, Willa, well played. Toby's mouth is wide-open in recognition of me, and all I can do is shake my head and glare in hope he gets the hint to not say a word. Luckily he does, sending me a wink. Most people here probably know exactly who I am, and I can only hope to distract her enough to not listen to any gossip.

"Well if you want to add to your excitement, I have clients over there on the blue sofa that are very open to fun adventures, especially with those they can take to bed. If that is something you are interested in?"

"Show us the way," Toby says. We head in that direction, and I lean down to tell Willia, "I only want to take you to my bed." I think my new favorite thing is making her blush and to feel her skin heat up when I know I have turned her on. Once I make introductions and Blake seems to be making conversation with Amity, I take the time to steal Willa away. I find us a cozy spot in a large red chair in the corner, away from the club's chaos. Taking full advantage of this unexpected time I have with her.

"You look hot as hell tonight. As soon as I spotted you, I thought I was going to have to fight those guys off."

"Mmmm, jealous, I like that," she murmurs as she literally boops my nose and giggles. A tale sign she is at least tipsy.

"How many of those have you had tonight?"

"Oh, BDSM. This is like my fifth one. Don't worry, I have a safe word when I can't take anymore."

FUUCKKK! I grunt as I run my hand down my face to not let her see the sinister look in my eyes. "Willa, I am going to need you to stop talking like that, unless you want me to handle you." Her face lights up, and she flaunts her own sinister grin, as she places her hand on my chest and runs it down my button up shirt and back up again.

"Not saying I am that kind of girl, but for you, Cowboy, you can have me whenever and whatever way you want. Just say when." Then she brings her hand up to my neck and strokes the back of it with her fingertips.

I let out a low groan. "Willa."

"Nash," she whispers back.

"What is your safe word, baby?"

She gives me her biggest grin and leans down to whisper in my ear, "More."

"More?" I question back, taking a low deep breath.

"With you, it is more, because I don't need a safeword with you." She moves her leg to the other side of me, to where she is now straddling me in the chair.

"You sure about that, baby?" I hum as I wrap my arms tighter around her waist, pulling her closer to me so her face is mere inches from mine.

"I am. For whatever reason and barely knowing you, I feel safe with you. And I also know, I would do anything you asked me too without question or concern. So yes, more, please." I am done as my hands reach through her hair and pull her lips to mine. Her tongue slides over mine, and she tastes like the best drink. Bourbon and cherries that I find perfectly fitting for her. After a few more sucks and bites followed with kisses in between, she pulls back.

"I just want to wrap your braids around my hand to hold you in place while I fuck you from behind." Her eyes instantly tell me she is more than willing to indulge. "To make you moan and scream my name."

"Not much of a screamer, Cowboy."

"You will be by the time I am done with you." I slide my hand between her legs and against her jeans, then back around to grab her ass, pushing her down on my hard cock. She bends down to kiss me again, and I ravish her lips, down her neck to her clavicle, as she lets another small moan. I pull back to catch her sexy, flushed face looking at me like she could burn me alive. I just might let her. We are a coil of arousal that needs to be unleashed.

"I do believe I need to punish you for your little alarm prank."

Willa hums in my ear, "Please do, Sir. Would it be by belt, whip, or your hand?"

"Jesus, is there somewhere I can take you now?"

"I would hate to mess up this designer suit of yours."

"Fuck Armani. You are worth it. Worth it all." I tell her as I hold her face in my hands, making sure she sees the sincerity in my eyes when I say that. At this point, I am not sure how we were ever strangers, because right now, it seems she has been here all along. Against all I have known and the full need to dominate, my inner being is caving. Allowing... more so wanting Willa to be in control. The familiarity of her welcomes the intensity she throws at me, bending my beast to relinquish all control.

Chapter 9: Fireball

Damn, that man can kiss and make me feel alive. The most alive I have felt in a long time if ever. Every time I tempt him, I feel him twitch under me, and his jaw clenches as if it is taking all his will power to hold back.

Just from the short time of knowing him, I can tell he prefers, no, more like needs to be in control. His honey-whiskey, swirly eyes tell me what I need to know. That is knowledge that I am now knowingly lusting over. Nash's words and voice are a stimulant to my body, and Hades help me when he darts his tongue through his lips when he looks at me with heavy lids of desire.

Before we have sex in this very public space, we agree to grab some food, more drinks, and chat for a bit. We moved closer in, so he could keep an eye on his clients, and I was intrigued to see Amity and Blake still hitting it off and taking fireball shots.

Lana and her fiance, Justin, are chatting it up with another couple we know, as well as Tilly being

Knowing they are all well and distracted, I feel less burdened turning my attention to Nash as we sit together telling life stories, learning one another, and laughing. Leaning across from him to grab the tabasco sauce for my quesadilla, he gently grabs my right wrist and runs his thumb over a scar.

"What is this from?"

"A broken beer bottle," I say, hoping that is enough to drop it.

"Another rowdy night or bar fight?"

"Bar fight would be a much cooler story…..To be honest, you probably don't want to know."

"I do. I want to know every inch of you, Willa–the good and the bad. Honesty will be the best for us."

"Um okay….I did warn you. I was dating this guy Brooks a couple of years ago. It was great at first, but then, at some point, something flipped in him. This scar is from one of those nights."

"Tell me everything," he barks out. I take a deep breath, not wanting to relive this moment of my life, but Nash has a pull to him for when he asks for something, my mind and body ask how high in terms to please him.

"Um..Well, the first time was taken as an accident. Because the thought of him putting his hands on me was unthinkable, and he was extremely apologetic afterwards. The second time happened a few months later, after we had a late night out, both drunk, and I was yelling at him because he was flirting with some chick. Wasn't even a slap, but a full fledged punch to the jaw. Left a small scar right here under my jaw line." I stop and rub my finger over the puckered flesh. " I took the blame and shame with me that time, thinking I egged him on. The third time was only two weeks later, he pushed me into my bedroom door and had his way with me and left." I can see Nash's jaw tensing as he keeps rubbing his thumb across the scar on my wrist.

Looking at him for some assurance, he tells me to go on. "Fourth time, I cannot even remember what he was pissed about, but had gotten smarter about it. He punched me on the inside of my thigh multiple times until it was swollen, black, and bleeding. Telling me that he wanted to make sure I did not forget about him while I was traveling for the rodeo. That sucker took forever to heal because I have to squeeze my legs to push my horse faster.

Happened right in the middle of the College National Finals. After that, I decided to leave him and moved back to my place. Tilly and Lana helped me, but he found me a few days later after we had all thought he was fine with me leaving. Dragged me out of my own bed in the middle of night, while holding a beer bottle in his hands. As I was pleading with him to stop and just leave, he cracked the bottle on the doorframe and sliced my wrist open. Blood was everywhere, which seemed to piss him off even more. So after he slapped me a few times, he threw my head aslantly at the coffee table. Dirks, my brother, luckily had heard commotion of a truck coming down the driveway and called the cops, but by the time he and the cops got there, I was already knocked out cold. Brooks was arrested, and I filed a restraining order. I had a solid concussion, left with a scar on my head, and this pretty little scar to remember it all by. Other than my girls, my family, those that helped, and Brooks, no one else really knows what happened."

"Where is this prick now?"

"Last I heard after he served his few months in jail because his daddy knows people, he moved to Tennessee. Haven't heard from him since that night."

"Who is he related to?"

"Please don't do anything, really." He nods his head to acknowledge my plea. "His dad is the mayor of Taylor. I won't go into detail how deep those lines of communication run in this state and all over." Nash nods again with an angst expression, as if knowing exactly who I was talking about. "Please leave it to rest."

"I will, I promise," he murmurs as he kisses the inside of my wrist. "Willa, there is...."

"Shots for everyone!" Amity shouts while carrying a tray of fireball shots and surrounded by everyone one we know at this point. Followed closely by Tilly with another tray.

Looking at Nash, who flashes me his sexy grin, we grab our shots and throw back, and then again.

~~~

Once things calmed down after taking several shots alongside more BDSMs and dancing until my feet hurt, we were finally resting again. I found that Nash has more control over his alcohol intake than I do. He can say no very easily, where I evidently cannot. Also, he is a drink then down some water do-er. It was not until at least an hour ago when he convinced me to only start drinking water. Blake had already left with Amity, and so had my other girls. Nash's clients seemed to hit it off with Toby and Eric, so it has been a long while since I have seen any of them.

"Can I take you home?"

"I don't want you going out of your way, especially this late at night. Also, you literally live right down the street, don't you?"

Nash nods. "At least let me have Grant take you home. Please, I would feel much better knowing you are not in a car with a stranger this late."

"And to think, how ever did I survive before I met you?" I laugh as I pat his cheek and smile.

"Let us not discuss your past rebel menacing ways right now."

"Okay, Sir. Your driver can take me home."

"Thank you," he replies and leans down to kiss me on the cheek. "I will walk you out to the car." Once placing me in the car with Grant, he tells me to text him when I get dropped off.

"Grant, who is this man named Nash?"

"I am not sure what I can say, Miss, but he is a respectable, driven, determined, and caring young man. Who seems to fancy you very much."

"Well I fancy him too." I say right before I fall asleep on the ride home.

Grant wakes me up and helps me to my door to ensure I get in okay. I even notice him checking all the rooms just to make sure I am safe. Then he pulls a small green bottle out of his pocket, and I know exactly what it is.

"You two are something else, Grant.... Something else." He smiles and closes my front door behind him. After I lock it, I send Nash a text.

Me: Sir, I have made it home safely by your impeccable driver, Grant. Also, thank you for the gift of hangover juice. Going to pass out and dream about you all night. XOXO

Nash: Good Night. Sleep well XXX

Chapter 10: Clover

    Thanks to Nash's mystery hangover concoction, I was able to be a functional human being this morning at school. Better yet, it was an early release day due to the boys basketball team heading to finals. So, now, here I am, standing in the barn looking at my handsome Paint, Ringo, debating whether or not I am going to jump on him for a ride or dwell on it. Last weekend was huge after I got on Doc and even rode around the arena once with a little girl who was scared of riding on the back of Betty. Being that Betty is an older red mare and probably the gentler and slower of the horses, it felt like a good second move. Now, I need to start making more moves in the direction that gets me back on a horse and racing. Not only does the rodeo team need me, and the fact that I feel a piece of me is lost, but I just got an invitation for an endorsement by the BBR American for the March show in Fort Worth. This a huge deal and one only a buffoon would pass up. If I accept that, I have three weeks to get myself and Ringo here ready.

"Clover is set up. You ready?" Tilly hollers behind me as she walks in.

"I really don't have a choice, do I?"

"Not if you want to take up that endorsement and hopefully ride it through qualifying for the American again."

"Right," I sigh as I feel defeated but place my hat on my head and climb on top of Ringo.

"Deep breaths, girl. We are going to take it slow until you feel more at ease. Dirks has been working with him and says he has a lot of speed and great balance around the barrels. Release him at the turns with pressure from your legs. He is a little different from Doc, where you are going to want to hold him back in between to rev him up more. At least until this becomes a routine for him. Full release on the straight line, and he will send it. Got it?"

"Got it. Slow and easy..... Here we go," I mutter as Tilly leads us out to the arena where the setup is. I see Dirks off to my left, standing up on the gate, ready to be there for what I may need. I take Ringo in, and we slowly dredge our path and circle around the barrels a few times until we both feel somewhat confident with each other. After the fourth time, I am feeling more relaxed, and we pick up a canter. Damn, this horse is bendable and strong. He really is a beauty and hugs the barrels at the center, I can only imagine what he is going to be like at full sprint. We take a quick break to grab some water.

"Looking good out there, sis."

"Trying. I need to see what happens when I push him."

"You think you are ready for that today?"

"No, but I need to. We are on a tight deadline, and I have to respond to Henry about the endorsement by Monday afternoon. So no time is wasted. Let's do it." I say while getting Ringo lined up at the gate, whispering a few prayers under my breath to not psych myself out.

Tilly shouts, "I got the timer. Ready?"

"Ready!"

"BEEP!" she shouts, the noise deafening to my ears.
Ringo takes off like he has done this a million times over again. Me, I am hanging on, but release his reins and squeeze as we come to the first barrel, then slowly pull back right before the second one, and he bends right around it, and the same for the third. Soon as we round the third barrel, I pull back just a bit and then let him go. Ringo hauls ass to the

open gate and comes to a complete halt when I ask him too.

"Good boy," I coo while scratching his neck. "Good boy, Ringo."

Tilly and Dirks walk over. "Well, you got 16.53. Not bad, not great, but I can also tell you are still pretty tense out there."

"Agree. Doc and I had down 14.17 before he got hurt, but that took us time to get there. I believe I only need to beat 16.21 in Fort Worth, based on who I saw was already registered." I feel my phone buzz in my pocket so I check real quick to see it is Nash calling. Knowing I need to focus, I send him to voicemail and line Ringo and I up to go again. Four more times around, we landed on 16.38. It will do for now, but I will take the win today of just being able to get out here and ride. To let loose again and push the both of us.

We all turn to see a black SUV come down the drive, and I jump off of Ringo, thinking I have a feeling of who is behind the wheel. Passing off Ringo to Dirks to untack, I head over to the car and low and behold I see Grant step out.

"Hi, Grant. What can I help you with?"

"I came to drop this off, along with these." Grant hands me a small velvet box and bouquet of stunning wildflowers.

"Thank you, Grant. Or should I say thank you to Nash?"

"All Nash. I am just the delivery boy," he says, chuckling.

"Well, I would hug you, but I am covered in dirt and sweat."

"No worries, Miss Willa.....You looked good out there. I caught the last ride when I was pulling in."

"Thanks. It has been a long time coming, but I'm glad to be officially back in the saddle." I hear him let out a "huh" under his breath and looks to want to ask more, but instead, he tells me goodbye, and that he would see me soon. I just wave back with my empty hand. Placing the box in my pocket, I head to the barn to help with Dirks before heading back to my cabin.

~~~

Finally made it back to my cabin post dinner with my parents. As I am undressing to hop in the shower, the velvet box falls out of my pocket onto the floor. *Shit!* I forgot all about it and have not even called Nash back. Running through the kitchen to grab my phone, I Facetime him. *Please pick up!*

"Hi Beautiful. It seems you are alive and well....and practically naked."

"Hey. Sorry.... A lot was happening today, and then after Grant stopped by I got busy with the barn and then had dinner with my parents."

"I am just giving you a hard time. Grant said he saw you riding today, and I told him I was jealous because I have yet to see this for myself."

"Well, it is a long story, but what he saw was not my best. But pushing to get there again. So you did not miss much."

"You going to tell me this story?"

"I will eventually. Oh, and I am not naked, I do have a sports bra on and panties." With that, I watch Nash's face tense with a flexed jaw as I slowly move the phone camera down my body with my black bra and pink lace panties.

"Death, just take me now," he mutters, running his hand through his dark locks.

"So dramatic," I say, laughing. "Speaking of Grant. Thank you for the gorgeous flowers. They are perfect and so much better than roses. And let me open this little box while I have you on the phone."

"You are welcome, Beautiful. I hope you like it."

Sitting my phone against the flower vase so he can see me open it, I undo the bow and slowly open the box. *I gasp, running my fingers over the platinum horse charm with a red hearted diamond on its chest.* "Nash, this is stunning. I can't…. There is no way I can accept this." It is simply exquisite.

"You are going to kind of have too. Turn it over."

My eyes widen as I read the back engraving, 'Ride baby Ride' with the Initials of NMH. "I take it those are your initials to this unknown last name." I see him nod.

"It is yours, and besides, I do not know any other badass cowgirls. Especially any I want to spend time with."

"Stop being such a smooth talker. Seriously though, thank you. I will add it to my bracelet." Gently putting it back in the box, I debate in my head if I will actually add it on because it looks too expensive to dangle on my arm.

"I see that face. Wear it. If you lose it or it falls off, we can get a new one."

"You are too much, Nash. Don't go spoiling me. I am not that kinda girl."

"Trust me, Willa. I know you are not, and that is one of the things I appreciate the most about you. I saw something that caught my eye today, and I knew the perfect person for it."

This man makes me grin ear to ear. Makes me have thoughts and feelings I have never had before, and oh my Hades, it has just been a week. Nash has knocked my guard down. My mind has all certain thoughts on it and uneasiness. My heart on the other hand, isn't looking back and ready to leap along with my female parts that ache for him.

We talk for another hour about our days before I realize I am the one falling asleep on the phone and still need to take a shower. After multiple attempts of goodbye, he hangs up, and I stay laying on my couch in a blissful mood as I decide just to go to sleep where I am at.

CHAPTER 11: DATE

I drive up to the cabin that Grant told me was hers. I had a feeling she would prefer to meet me up at the main house, but I am trying to avoid the parentals due to the oil situation because I have no doubt they will know exactly who I am, being the spitting image of my father and grandfather. My heart is not willing to take the chance of this relationship being doused before I can truly spark a beginning, especially after the other night. A lustful night I have jerked myself off too, more times than I can count in the shower.

Being early is a habit of mine, so as I make my way out of the truck and to her front door, I am curious how off guard I am going to catch her.

Knock, knock, knock

"Come in!" I hear Willa shout. I open the door, and a deep growl is released from me as I spot her bent over at the waist at the refrigerator with only black lace barely covering her ass cheeks. When I clear my throat, she shoots up and turns around, blessing me with the sight of her perfect, natural, plump breasts in a matching black lace bra.

"Oh my Hades and Zeus, I thought you were Tilly stopping by.....um hold on. Let me find my robe." I see her sprint into her room while hearing a few curse words under breath and then her running back through the room I am standing in. At the same time, we both spot her blue satin robe laying on the back of the couch, so I pick it up and hold it out as she walks over and slides her arms through the holes. Turning around, merely inches from my body, I catch a better glance of her body as she ties her robe together. Her cheeks are flushed as if she is not sure she is turned on by the *I want to fuck you* look or embrarrssed by what just happened.

"Hi," she squeaks, looking up at me.
Clearing my throat again and trying to calm my lower member down, I smile. "Hey, yourself."
She opens her mouth then closes it, while she gives me a look as if questioning something, then she asks, "Two things. I believe you are early, and I gave you my parents' house address, so how did you get here?"

"Yes, I am early because I prefer to be early. And yes, you did, but Grant told me what cabin you reside in."

"Okay, just wanted to make sure that was cleared up. I will have words with Grant at some other time."

All I can do is chuckle at her seriousness. "Are you upset with me?"

"No, just completely caught off guard along with showing you my goods." She blushes as she lets a little giggle out—that is the cutest thing I have ever heard.

Grabbing a hold of her robe, I yank her closer to me. "I appreciated the show more than you know. My mind has been racing with the scenes I want to play out with you, everywhere I want to touch you, to kiss you, tease you." I rub my hands up the sides of her body to her neck then face. I run my fingers through her hair as I lean down to whisper in her ear, "I look forward to the next time when you fully show your goods, so I can take the time to find your hidden tattoo." I slowly pull away as her face turns to mine.

Our eyes lock, and with that, before I can move, she is on her toes, wrapping her arms around my neck, pulling my mouth to hers. I take all of her as her tongue intertwines with mine, stealing her breath as if she has been starving for me and me for her. She tastes like the sweetest juiciest cherry I have ever sucked on and eaten. Willa moans slightly into my mouth, and I lose it. Pulling her up to wrap her legs around my waist, I walk to the nearest wall and push her against it. Us grinding onto each other as she pulls at my hair, and we both struggle to breathe but not wanting to let up. Undoing her robe, my hand slides up her bare skin when it stops on her right breast. Like I said before, her breasts are the perfect size for my large hands. Her right breast fits in the palm of my hand as I tenderly squeeze and tweak her nipple under her lace. She moans louder now as she grinds up against my hard cock that is in full attention.

Fletcher's continuous bark brings me out of our state, and as I slowly pull back, I tug on her bottom lip as I go, while I hold her face in my palms.

"That was incredible, but it would only be a gentleman like me to take you on a proper date before I take full advantage of you."

Trying to catch her breath, she murmurs, "Yes, so gentlemanly of you, Cowboy." She pats my chest. "Let me finish getting ready. Help yourself to the bathroom to clean up as well."

Nodding, she slips from my grasp, and I head to her bathroom. It sits between the kitchen area and her bedroom and smells just like her. I look in the mirror and see her lipstick has rubbed off on my face a bit, and my hair is a complete tousled mess now. After adjusting my lower-self, I bend down to the cabinet under the sink to grab a hand towel. I spot bottles of honeysuckle vanilla shampoo and lotions along with her leather cleaner. This is why she smells like the perfect garden. Standing back up, I begin to scrub the lipstick off of me and fix my hair. Also, I splash some more cold water on my face just to calm myself down. That was *Hot,* and she is sexy as hell, and that fucking moan of hers; I was mere seconds from coming in my pants.

Walking out, I am graced with cowboy boots and a short strapless dress, that leads me to believe she no longer has a bra underneath. She winks at me, and I shake my head back at her, laughing.

"You are trying to kill me aren't you?"

"Of course not, Cowboy. At least not until I have my way with you a few times."

"A few, huh?" Placing my hand on the small of her back, I steer her toward the door. "Let's go before I do all the bad things I want to do to you." Already knowing, all my *honest* plans of talking tonight just went out the window.

She walks in front of me out the door, but I feel her skin heat up under my palm at her back. The three of us load up in my truck, and we head off to SA for the start of date night.

Chapter 12: Guacamole

Fletcher sat between us the whole ride into town, but it did not stop Nash from putting his arm across the back rest and finding my shoulder to place his hand on. He kept giving my shoulder gentle squeezes as if to let me know he was there and to make sure I was okay. I won't lie, my body is still calming down from our impromptu makeout session. That was all levels of steamy, and I would have given myself to him right there had we kept going. But, thanks to Fletcher over here, he completely pussy blocked me.

After seven months of not having any fun, except with my BOB, she is ready. I am ready. So ready to see what lies underneath this man's clothes because what I felt through them has my thighs clenching together as we drive down the road.

Once we pull in a parking garage, I notice we are near the Riverwalk.

"Hope you are in the mood for some authentic mexican," Nash says as he holds his hand out to help me down from his truck.

"Is there any other?" I ask, smiling.

"Have you ever had Panchitos?"

"Can't say I ever have. Usually not on this side of the river when I come over here."

"Well, then you are in for a treat. Family owned, and some of the nicest people you will ever meet."

"Then lead the way, Cowboy." Taking my hand in his, we stroll up to the restaurant, and my mouth begins to salivate with all the smells of grilled steak and chicken with all the spices.

"Nash, how are you, son?" I hear as I see a happy, larger Spanish woman walking over to us, then wraps Nash in her arms. "It has been a long time since you came to see me."

"Not only did I come to see you, Lita, I brought someone with me." As he pulls back from her, he reaches for my hand and pulls me next to him. "This is Willa, Lita."

"Ohhhh, mujer hermosa. Willa, welcome to Panchitos. It is our pleasure to serve the two of you tonight."

"Thank you," is all I can say before she pulls me into her arms for a hug that I choose to reciprocate. I already feel this woman's genuine love in my soul. As she pulls back, she speaks to Nash in Spanish, which he clearly understands and speaks. I of course stand there smiling my little heart out because not an ounce of Italian I learned in school is going to help me in this conversation.

Soon, she leads us to a table that is inside but overlooks the lighted covered patio that looks out on the hill country in the far off distance. I am already loving how this view is not obstructed like the rest of downtown San Antonio and Riverwalk. As we take our seats, with Nash across for me, this Lita person turns back to me and places her hand over her heart and sighs. Again, I smile as she walks away. I look at Nash for a clue.

Lightly chuckling, he says, "That was my Lita. Or Rosa. I should say our families go way back, and though Rosa is of no blood relation, she has always treated my brothers and I as her own. So my brothers and I call her Lita. Meaning Grandmother in Spanish." Nodding my head, I am slowly catching on. "I bet you were wondering what we were talking about?"

"It would be nice because I am probably one of twenty people that took a whole other language other than Spanish."

Smiling now, he bobs his head back and forth as he stares at me. "Let me guess, French?"

"No, Italian. I took French for one semester, but had the opportunity to head to Italy one summer to ride, so I switched and so glad I did."

"That makes sense. Other than asking how my parents and brothers were doing, which one was here just last week, multiple times with a different woman on his arm each time, she was praising me on how beautiful you are. That she senses you are a cool-headed red head, not like those crazy ones I keep hearing about. That when she hugged you, she could tell you have a gentle but broken soul that needs healing and that maybe...."

Nash goes quiet on me, and I am somewhat stuck on the whole crazy red head part, it seems like there is something more important to be said. "That maybe...."

"That maybe, we could heal each other."

"Hmmm, okay. You look far from broken to me, but I also know how to mask it very well myself. Sensible woman over there, though, makes me nervous that she could tell by just being close to me."

"She believes she can see to your soul through those ice castle blue eyes of yours."

"Do you believe you can see my soul when looking into my eyes?" I ask him.

With him staring straight back, he says, "I know I can see your inner beauty in them, that you have bewitched me with them, and that there is a hint of sadness in them even when you have a smile on your face."

"Damn, Cowboy, you sure know how to make a gal blush."

Placing his hand over mine, he murmurs, "Enough of the heavy talk for a bit. Tell me, Willa, what do you do when you are not working at the ranch or teaching?"

"Oh, safe question.....I–" Rosa brings over two margaritas with some chips, salsa, and my favorite, guacamole. Once I see that it is the perfect consistency and all fresh, I begin to dig in. Completely distracted from what I was about to say. Nash looks at me in astonishment. "I'm sorry, do I need to share this with you?" I ask, laughing and covering my mouth that is full of chips and guac now.

"Not at all, baby, not at all. I will gladly get my own, as seeing you this happy with your own bowl of guacamole makes this moment memorable."

"Huh, that is similar to what my friend Lana says because that is what my granny always told us. Have memorable moments and cherish them. Even better if you can capture them on film. She was all about pictures and videos because she knew she would eventually grow old like her parents did and forget everything. Unless she had pictures to share to jog the memory. I was lucky to have her for as long as I did, and I know she had to have been the one looking out for me on the day of my accident."

"My grandmother tells us the same thing. That is so crazy. Maybe it was a generational thing. Because that is her favorite line to give us. Care to talk about your accident?"

"Nah, rather not spoil a perfect evening with sad stuff. Maybe some other time." I pop another guac filled chip in my mouth, stopping myself from even going there.

"I respect that. It seems we both like to shield others from our scars." All I can do is nod at that statement, thinking of the one that runs down my hip then my upper thigh, the small one down my ankle along with the open wound I still have on my heart that I am not sure will ever heal up if I cannot push myself to ride fully again. I need to change the conversation before I decide to down this margarita and have him see the crazy redhead I can be.

"Oh, so back to your original question. I am getting back to competing myself, post accident. I actually got a sponsorship for an upcoming event so I can start to qualify for the American." Nash gives me a grin and looks completely lost, so I dive into details about the events I compete in, what the American is and how great the sponsorships are.

He asks questions about my time, if anyone can sponsor, my placings, and winnings. I am unable to hold my grin when he tells me how much he is impressed with my accomplishments, and that I am the coolest girl he has ever met. Without saying much about the accident, I do speak on how I spent all my savings to save Doc Holiday and the financial strain I am in now. The sponsorship helps cover the entry fees and hotel accommodations if I need them. I just have to get my horse and I to the place.

If nothing is ever more embarrassing, crying on your first date to a striking, dapper, gorgeous man who is opulent about being so thankful for the sponsorship and thankful for my horse, family, and being able to ride again. He comes over to sit next to me and hugs me, kissing the top of my forehead, where no words are needed. No words to know that he truly cares for me and nothing else has ever felt more natural in my life other than riding a horse. Wiping my eyes as Rosa begins to walk over, he moves back to his side of the table.

"So, Nash, care to enlighten me of your last name yet, and what you do for a living that affords you the lavish lifestyle it seems you have?" I catch a quick glance of panic in his face before he straightens up and pulls a poker face on me. During this time, Rosa has brought out more guacamole, fajitas that are sizzling with immense heat and spice, along with all the sides of rice, beans, the shredded queso cheese, and lettuce. She even brought out Fletcher his own plate of steak and chicken.

Leaning down to scratch his ears, I whisper, "Why do I get the feeling you eat better than me most days?"

Nash's laughs as he hears me. "He eats better than most people I know, that is for sure."

We both begin to fill our tortillas up with all that has been laid out before us, and as I begin to fold mine up, I look up at him. He seems to be concentrating hard as I can see a slight shake in his left hand. Turning my eyes away, I just say, "I'm waiting, Cowboy."

"Do I really need to?"

"Dude, I have been like an open book with you answering your Q&A and just cried in front of you, which I really hate myself for right now.. Besides you said you would let me know on our date. So I have been waiting."

"I honestly never had anyone 'dude' me before." He looks over at me as I take a giant bite and smiles. "You are the most refreshing thing in my life right now, Willa."

"Oh," I say with a surprised look on my face.

"I mean that as a compliment. You are stunningly beautiful but do not seem to recognize it or even care for that matter. For the most part, you say what is on your mind, food brings you joy, which for most women these days is not a thing. It seems you can hold your own in a tough crowd, which we will be coming back to in a bit. I just wanted you to know that. To hear that from me because this is all new to me, and I feel like a literal fish out of water, but I really like you, Willa. Since the moment you stumbled your way inside my suite, I have thought of nothing else. I went from having no idea who you were to now, I want to know everything about you. Because there is something between us, and I know you feel it too. So please take that for what it is worth to you, based on what I am about to tell you."

"It is worth a lot, Nash. My feelings are the same, and I am very much into you. So I am listening."

He takes a deep breath and holds my hand in his across the table. I won't lie, his hand holding is keeping me from attaching that fajita I just created, but I guess it can wait.

He takes a deep breath. "My last name is Holdings.... As in Holdings Oil Company. I am also the CEO of the company." I can feel his hand squeeze a little tighter around mine as if he needs to make sure I do not want to walk away from this right now. I just look at him in shock. I know damn well who the Holdings are, and how the hell did I miss that the guy across from me is like the most wanted bachelor along with his brother Clint? Oh shit.... How did I not see any of this?

"I swear, Willa, I had no idea who you were until you sent me your address the other night. I am personally not forthcoming with my last name as I have learned people are not genuine and would rather use my family name and money for their own gain. Please say something."

I can tell quickly he is genuinely pained by this conversation, but I do manage to slide my hand out from his, only for him to give me a defeated look. Looking at him, I say, "I believe you, Nash. I do. But what now? Last I heard, my family hates the Holdings name and what your company stands for. And maybe not all of it, because I get it, you are providing us oil, but also helping yourself and others get rich. The Holdings have been after my family's land for years. My family's property is off limits, Nash, regardless of who we are to each other. Unless you are willing to walk into my parents home, explain who you are, and promise to never speak of oil being spilled out of our land again, there can never be an us. My family has fought too hard to keep your company and others like it away. Even when we have been at our poorest, giving in has never been an option. That ranch is their survival, it is for the wild horses we rescue, sanctioned land, it is home to a dozen or so other animals, and a vacation spot to others who want to experience the cowboy lifestyle. Most importantly to you, it is my home. Where I learned to rope and ride, where I fell off and got back on my horse, it is where I hang my hat at the end of a long day. To me it's home."

    I hastily gather my purse, pull out some cash, and throw it on the table. I quickly head to the bathroom to escape him from seeing my tears again. My heart is not breaking just because of who he is to my family, but because who he was becoming to me over this past week. I have never felt so much electricity, need, and want over someone my entire life. How do I ignore that?

    Damnit, if there isn't a line.

    Stuck in line, praying he does not come for me, I look at the photos on the wall, hoping to stop the tears from falling. A few of them catch my eye fairly quickly, leaving me even more dumbfounded. The first one is of my granny with a woman I am unsure of. Then I see another picture that looks like a younger Rosa, with my granny in it also and a whole other family. Wait, is that my grandpa? What the hell is going on here?

    I began to follow the rows of pictures of what looks like Rosa's family as well as Nash's family over the last decade or more. I soon stop over a picture that looks just like Nash in front of a huge army tank, decked in army gear from head to toe. He is smiling and looks like he must be with his squadron of about eight men and two women. Shit, he looks to be a Sergeant. That badge on the lower part of his sleeve looks just like the one my granny sewed in my grandpa's. It is not a typical army badge either.

With the knowledge I have from my own grandpa serving in the Army and being a Major General before he decided to finally retire to the ranch, I have so many questions, but I am not sure where to start as the bathroom finally becomes available, and I rush in.

CHAPTER 13: SECRET

Willa just left me at the table, and what is it with her throwing money down? I saw her run in the direction of the bathroom, so I have some time to figure out my next move. I am stunned she did not even let me say a word before she took off, but I also completely understand the feeling of how can this, us, be. My Lita came over and hugged me, saying she saw and heard all, but to give Willa time. Nodding my head as if I understood, I knew I could not give Willa time. Any time away from her left my brain in a fog and unable to concentrate. So I walk over to the bathroom door and wait for her to come out.

Ten minutes later she finally does, swinging the door open, and her face is flushed from tears. "What, what are you still doing here? Did you not hear me last time? There is NO us, Nash."

Grabbing her by the wrist, I pull us inside the bathroom and push her up against the door. Holding her wrists above her head in one hand, I stroke my other hand down her face.

"Willa, there is going to be an us because that is how strongly I feel about there being an US. If you need me to talk to your parents I will. If you need me to tell my dad to shove it about your family's land, I will. I did not almost die once too come back here and be alone. Whatever you need me to do, to ensure there is an us, tell me, baby. Just tell me. You are worth it. There is this pull to you that I do not think I can break even if I wanted to."

She cries in my arms, "Why does this hurt so bad?"

"Because falling in love hurts." She looks unsteadily at my face and back down to her hand where I can see her turning a ring on her right index finger. I lean down to kiss her on top of her forehead. "I am so sorry I withheld this information from you. I needed to get my thoughts and emotions in order about you, about us. I swear I am not the villain here. Tell me, baby, tell me what you need from me?" I run my fingers through her fiery hair and back down her face. Her walking out without me is not an option.

"I need you to explain a few things to me," she whispers as she opens the bathroom door and pulls me into the hallway of pictures.

"Do you know how this is? " She asks as she points to a lady I remember seeing through family photos.

"I am not really sure, but I can tell you the woman next to her is my grandmother, and this other woman is in several pictures throughout my family albums. Why?"

"That other woman is my granny. And in this picture, not only do I see my granny, but also my grandpa, standing next to what I now know are your grandparents. What could this possibly mean? And is it a coincidence that you were in the Army the same as my Grandpa with that exact same badge?" She points out.

"I know nothing, Willa, I swear. I never cared to ask who else were in these pictures because I was young when we would go through photo albums of the past. And never really paid attention to what Rosa had hung up. I did not even know she had this picture. I know I had unknown connections that others always spoke about, so it pushed me harder to earn my place because I seemed to move up fairly quickly compared to fellow comrades," I say, pointing at the one from my time in the Army. "This badge was given to me as soon as I enlisted. My grandmother gave it to me and said it was from a dear friend who served." Stopping, I think over what we are looking at. "Come on, let us go talk to Rosa and see what she knows." Taking Willa by the hand, we head to the back of the restaurant to the office.

"I was wondering how long it would take the two of you to come find me," my Lita says.

"Well we are here now, so please share what you know, Lita." I plead. "Did you know who she was when I brought her in?" She nods her head to say yes. Willa sits down next to her and takes her hands into her own.

"Please, Rosa." Willa asks.

"I do not feel this is my story to tell, but I am not sure anyone left can tell the story more accurately than me. Of course I knew who Willa was as soon as she walked in because she looks just like her beautiful grandma, especially with that long red hair and those bright sky blue eyes. It skips generations therefore that is why your father has black hair like your grandpa. But you, my lovely, are a spitting image of your Grandma Ellie. I am sure you have been told that all your life, but it is true." Willa nods her head in agreement.

"Let me start from the beginning. Both of your grandparents were best friends growing up since I believe the age of six. Inseparable duo. I did not meet them until my twenties. Willa, I met your grandma first. We met on the army base we were living on with our husbands. Our husbands were in the same battalion, as we had just been transferred back to Texas from North Carolina. We were so happy to be back in our home state, but we still knew no one that far south. Ellie soon took me in as we sent our men off to war overseas. They were gone for months, with very little correspondence in between, so it was really hard, especially back then without all the technology we have now.

"Anyways, Ellie brought me into her inner circle that included your grandma, Nash. It seemed your Grandma Lainey was on base every weekend with Ellie or vice versa. So wherever they went, they brought me along. Ellie and Lainey were so much fun to be around, and everyone enjoyed being in their presence. Our men came home for a short stent, and at that time, Lainey had met your grandpa, Nash. Mr. Jacob Benedict Holdings himself. Already coming from a long line of old money and business in oil. He seemed to blend well with our group. They seemed so in love, and somehow, Lainey convinced him to pull off a quick extravagant wedding before our own husbands were shipped back overseas. Luckily Jacob's parents already loved Lainey as she came from an influential family herself. All about prestige back then.

"Fast forward many years later, Willa, your grandpa Henry had moved up the ranks as he felt that was his calling. He wanted to be the best while serving his country. My husband, Ricky, decided after the last tour they had, he was willing to stay on active duty but wanted to live a life as a civilian, so we found a small piece of land and started a family, with the dream of owning our own restaurant. With Ellie still being an army wife, Lainey and I grew closer, our husbands grew closer along with Jacob offering to be an investor to our dream."

Patting my hand, she continues, "We will always be the most thankful to your grandparents." Then she turns back to Willa. "Your grandparents bought that land after your grandpa became a lieutenant. On some vacation they had out west, Ellie fell in love with horses and the "easy" life she called it. She wanted her own dream, so with their savings, they bought the ranch so she had a place to make her dream a reality, and he would come home for a few weeks at a time or on weekends, depending on what was going on at the base. Us women became each other's family, sisters some would say. We helped her build what it was until your parents took over."

Lita pauses with grimace. "Unbeknown to any of us, everytime we were out there and Jacob tagged a long, he was taking soil samples from the land. There was a spot off the pond where oil had surfaced. Ellie had Jacob look at it because she was unsure, and he had told her it was nothing to worry about. It was just swampy mud from the pond running over during storms. She thought nothing of it, but Jacob kept it to himself. Push forward a year later, Jacob has a conversation with Henry over the land, letting him know there was oil there and begins to push him to sell so Jacob could start drilling.

Ellie was beside herself. She had finally gotten the place as she wanted, they had just purchased several horses and two cabins to build to rent out. Ellie also had the vision of a horse sanctuary. She wanted to rescue the horses that were being pushed off their land and sold off. So she was an admandt no, and Henry chose his wife's happiness over wealth. And he promised her never to go back on that. He wanted nothing more than to have her dream as he had his with his career and her. It gave her peace when he was stationed elsewhere. Henry knew if something ever happened to him, she would still have their home. It became a sore subject and was not talked much amongst us.

"Jacob did not come around as often, and over time, we all just settled within our busy lives, seeing each other every often. All of the kids were around the same age, so they were friends and went to school together, so that helped us stay together. Several years later, now we were in our late thirties, Henry and Ellie had a huge fight over their son, your dad, Willa, going into the Army, which found Henry over at the Holdings house and Ellie at mine. Jacob did not like that Henry and Lainey were so close, but they were because of Ellie. Jacob wanted to take advantage of it and threatened Lainey with divorce to take advantage of Henry in this delicate state. Him and Ellie never fought, but he felt strongly about sending your father in the army to serve his country like he did. Ellie wanted him to have a different life, and your father seemed to feel the same. It all is so sad and twisted, but Lainey felt she had no choice or she would lose everything, including her two children. Over the next month or so, she pursued Henry behind Ellie's back, and in a moment of weakness, Henry caved. Lainey gave him the answers that Ellie would not. She made him feel like a "man," that he was right about everything and boosted his ego. Sure enough, when he fell into bed with Lainey, Jacob was right there to pursue blackmail. He threatened to tell Ellie about the affair unless he sold the rights to that part of the land so he could drill. Talk about a small town scandal."

    Willa and I look at each other and realize this is not about oil, but our own grandparents' faults. That this is way deeper than we could have imagined.
Lita continues after taking a drink of water. "Henry was beside himself, and after punching Jacob out, Lainey confessed everything. They both went to see Ellie and told her what happened. I just so happened to be there, dropping off some food, and heard it all. Ellie was beside herself and kicked Henry out. Then determined as she was, turned around and blackmailed Jacob, said she would let everyone know what a shady businessman he was, using his wife to seduce men for oil plots. Threatened to run his family name in the ground and out of town. Jacob had no choice but to back down. As upset as she was with Lainey, she also

threatened that he would never leave her or their kids. To never do her wrong again or she would come for him." My brows hit my hairline at that. Ruthless. "With that, she cut all ties to the Holdings, and after a while, us too. She eventually took Henry back because she realized her heart hurt more without him then it would with him. She finally forgave him and that piece is history."

She laughs as she looks between us. "It is funny how your two dads grew up best friends, but after that, they never spoke again. Went off and did their own things and were cordial when they crossed paths. My little Selena and Luis were on the back end of it all.

They tried to remain friends with both, but over time, it seemed Nash's dad was the only one willing to remain friends with my kids. So we have stayed close to the Holdings. When Jacob passed several years ago, it was the first time I saw Lainey genuinely feel relieved and smile. Like she felt freed from her past, but I could tell her heart was still broken over losing Ellie. She even went to Ellie's funeral, standing off behind a tree. I have gone with her several times to visit Ellie's grave also. The same for Henry's. We were there, watching you grow up from afar, Willa." Grabbing my arm, she looks straight at me as she continues, "Back when your grandmother still had her wits about her, she used to talk about the two of you being together. Said she had dreams of if life had taken a different path. Of how they would have remained close until the end, while their kids and grandkids grew up together and maybe merge the two families. That would make her heart full because every Holdings needs a Bennett/Crenshaw in their life. Desperate to break the past. Because she knew what kind of lady you would be, Willa, and how Nash was being raised, that the two of you would be a match on fire if it ever happened. She has even prayed over Ellie's grave about it. Now look at the two of you."

Lita smiles, standing up to bring both of us in her arms for a hug. "Look, I am not sure what story either side knows or believes, but making them forgive and move past it will not be easy. It would be worth seeing if Lainey can speak to it because all she ever wanted was Ellie's forgiveness after all of it. And Lainey knew that Ellie threatened Jacob to never leave her. So she has always been thankful for that."

"Is it wrong that I really hate my dead grandfather now?" I growl.

"Oh, my neito, this was never to be your burden to carry. Forgive and move on. The outcome is now. This is what the two of you have control over. I know this makes my heart full, so I can only imagine what it would do for Ellie and Lainey. So please, do not let this pass. It is as if the divine has stepped in on their behalf."

We both hug her again and thank her and proceed to walk to my truck. Both not saying a word. Both not knowing how to tread this situation. The only thing I know is I am not losing this woman because of selfish past mistakes.

Chapter 14: Cherry

We are several minutes down the road, and I burst out laughing. I am hungry, no, correction, hangry, feeling betrayed in some kind of way, and Nash looks like someone just died. He must have heard my stomach rumble a few times because we are now pulling up to a Whataburger.

"This date is not turning out as I had planned. With all that going on back there, I did not even think to ask Lita to pack up some food to go. I knew I should have waited until the end of the night to reveal myself, but you asked."

"It is fine, at least Fletcher here ate." Smiling, I pat Fletch on his back, but I know good and well I am being a smartass. "Besides, you had no idea how I would react, plus, I am glad you did because the longer you would have waited, the more infuriated I would be. Also, we had Rosa to offer insight."

"Fair. Want to tell me why you were just laughing?"

"Because if I don't, I might just cry. Hey…. At least we did not find out we were blood related. I was worried we were entering 'Flowers in the Attic' terrority." He blinks his eyes at me as if questioning my sanity.

"You know, the book about the brother and sister that fall in love and sleep together?"

"I know it. Honestly, I am not sure if I am stunned that you have jokes right now, or threw us in the bucket of incest."

I can't help but laugh. "Again, laughing is better than crying. And come on, you can not tell me that was not going through your mind back there. I was on the edge of my seat the whole time, not sure what she was going to say next."

"It passed through my mind, but then I knew it could not have been because Lita would have been worried when she met you and would have said something sooner."

"Well glad you had some insight because it all came out of left field for me."

"Come on, let's go get something to eat, and we can discuss our next move on approaching this."

"Okay. Fair warning, I will not be sharing my fries with ketchup or Dr. Pepper shake."

He smiles, giving me a wink, while holding the door open for me. He obviously thinks I am playing around.

~~~

    Willa was not kidding. She does not share. I stole a fry, dipped it in her open ketchup then popped in my mouth, followed by a sip of her shake. Smirking at her, she only had her mouth gaped open long enough for me to imagine what it would feel like for it to wrap around my cock, but then her face went stealth.

    "You will pay for that," she states.

    Or at least I thought she was joking. That is until we jump back in the truck, and she pushes Fletcher over so she can sit next to me and play cock-tease. Subtly moving her hand up and down my thigh while driving down the road. She gets close to my hardness to just barely touch then moves her hand back down my leg. All while lightly kissing my neck that turns into nibbling. Sexual tension has always been there between us since we first met. She is pushing my limits to keep from tying her up and have my way with her.

    "If this is punishment, then by all means, Cherry, keep it up."

    "Cherry, huh?"

    "Yes, you always taste like one, and it seems to match your deep red hair." I turn to try and catch her mouth with mine quickly, only to be denied.

    "No touching, Nash." Willa lets out a low moan by my ear, and I feel it vibrate down my whole body.

    "Willa, you are dousing this fire in gasoline."

    "Well then, Cowboy, what are you going to do?" she whispers at the base of my throat, vibrating the sound through my core. I pull my truck over, and I'm thankful we are on a backroad to her place. There has never been a time I have let a woman play games with me, let alone aroused because of it.

    "This." Pulling her out of my truck and over my shoulder, I walk over to the right passenger side to lay her on the back bench seat. "Comfortable?" I growl out.

Her eyes glisten with desire, telling me her answer. In a movement, I rip her black lace panties off, and they fall to the ground when I hike her dress up over her hips. Taking a step back, I admire her beauty with her legs spread wide for me, already so wet and glistening for me to taste.

"Willa, I need to taste you." Not even waiting for her to answer, I bend down and take a long lap with my tongue from the bottom to the top of her clit where I flick her clit ring with my tongue. She lets out a soft moan.

"You are mouthwatering," I groan as I dive back into her pussy, confirming my suspicion that every part of her tastes like sweet ripe cherries. Licking and twirling my tongue in her while she moans, my hand pushes down on her pubic bone while flicking her clit ring. All of it making me groan and not sure I will not be coming in my jeans. This is what she does to me. Makes me completely undone and forget all logical sense. Point taken, with the current scene as we are on the side of the road where anyone can drive by at any moment. I don't care because I have to taste her, hold her in my mouth as my hands reach under her ass to squeeze her cheeks and pull her closer to mouth. Willa begins to buck against my mouth, and it is ravishing. She tightly grips my hair with her long fingers.

"Nash......Nash...."

"Just let go, my cherry, let go onto my tongue..... I got you." She moans loudly as I curl my finger up in her sex to feel her body quiver, coming down from her high. I continue to lap and lick her sweetness because it is utterly addictive.

"I have never had anything as sweet and delicious as you."

Pulling her dress back down to cover her, she leans up and pulls me to take my mouth to hers. Knowing she is tasting herself off my tongue by my doing is hot as fuck. I pull myself in the truck with her so we continue this makeout session. There is no getting enough of her. Never leaving my lips, she straddles my lap with her naked heat up against my hardness. My cock is already on the edge of exploding.

Out of breath, she expresses, "I don't want to have sex yet in the truck, but need to feel closer to you. Can we remove the jeans?"

"Anything you ask is always yours." Reaching down to undo my belt and jeans, she helps push them down to my ankles and off. When she climbs back onto my lap with only my boxer brief material between us is more than enough for me to lose it. Hands reach for her head with my fingers intertwined tightly around her hair, pulling her head back as I lick and suck on her neck, then guiding her back to my mouth as our tongues dance together. No words are needed while our bodies mold and grind together. Willa pushes her body down harder and rocks her hips faster. She is taunting and tantalizing all at once.

"Ride me, baby."

"Fuck," she whispers. "You are going to make me come again."

"You won't be alone. Harder," I growl back under my breath, pushing down on her shoulders to push her clit against me even more. Us both panting, kissing, starving for each other. This sends both of us over the edge as we come together. I take two of my fingers and wipe them between her folds then bring them to my mouth and suck. "I don't think I will ever get enough of how you taste, Willa."

"I hope not," she whispers, coming in for another kiss. Then she climbs off of me, and I feel her warmth go with her, only to bend down on the bench seat and remove my boxer briefs. She proceeds to lap me up and sucks my cock clean. Too soon, it springs back to life with not much coaxing.

"Holy shit, Willa! Were you made for me?" Pulling her mouth and twirling tongue off my length, she looks up at me with those icy blues.

"Yes, Sir, I am," she says huskily, then takes me back into her mouth and hits the back of her throat with my tip. As she moves her mouth up and down over me, I see her hand reach down to pleasure herself.

"Here let me help you." Inserting two fingers inside her pussy, she lets out a moan as if she just released the sweetest hum of melody down my length. She is already so wet and swollen again.

The animal in me feels primal that it is me who can get her this way, with barely touching her, with just my cock in her mouth. *Fuck.* Her tongue swirls around my tip and teases the slit before she takes me again in a long slow stride sucking hard.

"Good girl," I say, fisting her hair in my other hand as I continue to dip my fingers in and out of her. She moans, letting me know she likes being a good girl. Wanting to see how far she can go, I tell her to take me all in, over and over again, and she does as I tighten my grip on her hair to keep me from releasing down her throat. "Willa, come up here. If I cannot slip in you yet, I need to at least feel your body and taste you again." She nods as she continues to grind against my palm and lets out a sound of defeat when I remove my hand. "Trust me," I say as I pull her dress off over her head and meet with 2 perky breasts with pebbled nipples yearning to be felt and sucked. Which I do a few times, while kneading them. Her arching back gives me access to drag my tongue up and down her neck to chest. I then lay down on the bench seat. I am way to long for this, but fuck, this is what we both right now. "Willa, crawl on top of me with your cunt down to my face....That's it, lay on your stomach. Now you will suck my cock as I eat you pussy. Got it?"

"Yes, Sir," she purrs, causing my dick to twitch because this is fucking sweet heaven as I lick her between the folds, and she takes me back in to her mouth, coating me in her saliva. I spank her ass which sends a lethal moan through her, and she begins to grind against my mouth again. My pleasing Willa is now my stimulant. As much as she is enjoying her own pleasure, she never lets up on me, sucking harder and cupping me beneath spirals my control to nonexistent. I suck and lick her harder and deeper, with slaps to the ass in between.

"Willa…..Holy shit, Willa, I am about to….." Groaning into her backside, she pushes her cunt back to my mouth as she sucks and swallows my warm heat down. With one long lasting lick of her tongue, I tell her, "good girl," again and go back to having my tongue between her folds so she can fully enjoy the pleasure her body is pulsing with. She moans my name loudly as she orgasms against my mouth, and I lap her juices up as if she is the last sweetest cherry on earth. Leaving both of us panting against each other and longing to hold her, I have her turn around then pull her in my arms. I need to hold this fiery angel for a while. After a few minutes and a loud sigh from Fletcher that has us laughing, I say, "Let's get you home and clean up."

"Okay. And you might as well just stay the night, since we plan on talking to my parents tomorrow. Do you have any other plans?"

"I'm all yours, Cherry."

Smiling, she murmurs, "Well good. I will try not to wake you since I have to get up early and practice before the tourists make an appearance."

My brows furrow. "How early are we talking?"

"Early enough to not roll in the sheets all night," she says, giving me one of her many cute sultry faces.

CHAPTER 15: RIDE

I had the best ever sleep last night, all up until I heard a damn rooster crowing at the sunrise. Nothing happened once we got back to Willa's place. We showered separately and got ready for bed. Lucky for me, I always leave an overnight bag in my truck for emergency trips. I held her all night and rubbed her back with my fingertips until she fell asleep, with me right behind her. I am sure Fletcher appreciated the night of peace also. Now he and I are both wide awake, so I decide to get up and get dressed. Throwing some jeans on and a t-shirt, I walk in the kitchen and see a bag of dog food on the counter for Fletcher with a note.

Help yourself to some coffee. I ran up to my parents and grabbed some dog food for Fletcher. Not sure if this is what he eats or not, but I didn't want him to go hungry. Help yourself to whatever. Breakfast will be at the main house @8:00am if you can wait that long. I will be back by then to get you though.

XOXOX- Willa

Huh, how early did she get up? I didn't even notice her rolling out of bed. I must have been zonked out. I do some snooping on her shelves, looking at pictures, and books she has. I do notice some of her books turned backwards which bothers my OCD, so I pull them out to fix the issue. Glancing over the titles of billionaire CEOs, Alpha mates, and flat out gritty covers of shirtless men, I take a note, as this explains quite a bit about my fiery angel. It is one thing to read about and another to act on it. Grabbing one to throw in my bag to read up on later, I go back to fixing them her way.

Letting Fletcher out the front door to do his own business, I look over to my left, and I can see Willa on the back of a horse. Looks like a Paint from here. Thinking I am going to enjoy watching this, I head back to grab a cup of coffee, then sit back on the front porch in one of her rockers with Fletcher by my feet. I notice another guy down there with her, which I am guessing is her brother, Dirks, that she has mentioned to me.

Damn. She is incredible. I don't know anyone who can put their trust in a horse like that at full speed. For Willa, it looks effortless from where I am sitting. Rounding the barrels over and over again until she stops and jumps off the horse. I watch as the guy brings her a black horse, and she walks both of them around the barrels together, then she jumps on the black one. Wait, is there not a saddle on that horse? What in the hell is she doing? I would love to get a closer view, but not wanting to interrupt what she is doing, I decide to continue watching from the porch. I see her lean down like she is whispering something in the horse's ear, and the horse starts walking off. Willa puts her arms straight out to her sides in the air, and the horse picks up speed. *Shit!* Her ass is going to fall off. Does she have any sense when it comes to her well-being? Slipping on my boots, I start to walk down there, but as I get closer, I can tell she is smiling and laughing. The look of freedom. I continue to stare in wonderment. Who am I to tell her she is crazy for what she is doing? She lives this world, I don't. But I know the feeling of being part of something dangerous and on the edge, with everyone warning you to be careful. It's a choice.

I make it to the side of the fence and prop my boot up on the railing while leaning over it.

"Hey, man." I hear, turning to see the guy walk over. Extending his hand, he says, "I'm Dirks, Willa's brother."

Taking his hand in mine, I give a firm handshake. "Nice to meet you, Dirks. I am Nash." Taking a sip of coffee, I nod toward Willa. "She is really good at that."

"Good? She is a powerhouse in this world. Shame the accident took her out a bit, but looks like she is getting her groove back."

Looking back at Willa and deciding to play dumb because she has yet to tell me, I ask, "So that must be Doc she is on now and was part of the accident, right?"

"Yeah, man. They are both lucky to be standing and moving right now. I was right at the gate when it happened. Like her, I swear I heard Doc's ankle break. Knowing Willa was bad-off, all she could think of at that moment was making sure he was okay. I still have flashbacks of her laying there with blood matted in her hair and flowing down her face. As soon as we were able to move Doc off Willa enough to pull her out, when I went to pick her up, I heard and felt the snap of her hip bone. I almost dropped her when I froze, but Pa and the paramedics came over and took her. She was on so much adrenaline and worrying about Doc, she had no idea how broken her body was."

"Wow, sounds like an intense moment. Seems like she has come out on the other side alright."

"Up until last weekend, she would not even get on a horse. I might have you to thank for that. Tilly told me they walked into the barn with her on Doc, taking a picture for you."

Knowing exactly what picture he is speaking of, I hold back a smile. "Huh, she did not let on it was such a big deal."

"Tilly said she was in shock when she realized what she had done." Nodding my head, I take another sip of coffee, all while taking notes in my head that I know I am invading her privacy, but she has marked off as off limits. Not just the accident, she does not talk about much of this. Every time I ask her, it is a short answer like no big deal and moves on to another topic. Last night was the first night I actually got some information out of her. This is a big deal, she is an amazing deal.

"So the paint over there, who is that?" I point out the first horse Willa was riding.

"That is Ringo." I laugh to myself at another Tombstone name. Dirks continues, "That is who she is going to compete with. She burned through her entire life's savings and winnings to save Doc's life though he will never be her rodeo partner again. Those two were like lighting and could read each other's thoughts. I think she thinks if she has both of them in the arena together, Doc will share some knowledge with Ringo. Also, she finds her balance best on Doc, so she is hoping it will help her sense what is off when she is on Ringo." It is then I see her stand up on Doc's back as he trots around the arena.

"What the hell is she doing?" Putting my coffee cup on the ground, I'm about to climb over the fence when Dirks places his arm out in front of me.

"Breathe, man. This is nothing compared to some of the crazy shit she does. Those two would open up the rodeo with their stunts. When you have a minute, search for *Sequins in Tombstone* video. It will blow your mind." Not taking my eyes off of Willa, I watch her calmly sit back down as she makes her way to us.

"Morning, Cowboy, did I wake you?"

"No, your rooster did. But you about gave me a heart attack with those stunts of yours." She laughs as I look up at her on her horse. Camo ball cap on with her hair in 2 braids, a gray shirt in jeans with her boots all while the sun peaking over her head. "God you are gorgeous." A clearing of a throat brings me out of my insistent staring.

"Okay, Cowboy, let's work on getting you fed."

"Tilly and I can untack Ringo and release them both back out," Dirks speaks up.

"Thank you, bro. I'll see y'all at breakfast then."

I decide to pick Willa up in a bridal style and carry her back to the house. "Nash, I am getting you all smelly and dirty. You need to put me down."

"Too late, damage is done. Is this better?" I smirk as I throw her over my shoulder, slapping her ass.

"You win."

"That's what I thought." As we reach her front porch, I swing open the screen door and walk in, slowly letting her slide down the front of my body. Placing my palms on both sides of her face, I lean down to kiss her. "You are the most incredible, challenging, brave, and beautiful person I have ever met Willa." She blushes, putting her hands on my wrists, pulling my hands off her face.

"Thanks Nash. Just an average girl here."

"There is nothing average about you, baby. I promise whatever transpires over the next few hours, days, what it may be, I am not letting you go. You are the only thing in my life worth keeping."

Reaching up on her tip-toes to kiss me, deflecting, she says, "I am going to jump in the shower, joining me?"

"Yes, give me two, and I will be there."
She walks off, and I need to call Clint because I noticed I missed his call earlier.

"Hey, man, what's up?"

"We have a problem, brother."

"What could it be on a Saturday?"

"Mom and Dad are back. Got in last night. It seems they caught wind of their favorite son hanging out with a red head. Pictures too."

"What the hell? What pictures?"

"A handful from the concert, you on the phone on the golf course, smiling, and then a few heated ones from Thursday night."

"Who keeps following me, that I don't know?"

"You know you are like the hottest bachelor in Texas, you cannot be in shock over this."

"Not in shock, just pissed about this shit. Do Mom or Dad know who she is yet?"

"They didn't say much, but I hope you plan on meeting up for a family dinner tonight."

"Fuck. Fine. I need to go. I'll check in later."

We say bye, then I throw my phone onto the couch, needing to put my poker face before I strut in her bathroom.

Opening the door, the steam has fogged up the mirror and glass doors. Willa swipes her hand around the glass so I can see her through the water drops. I catch a glimpse of her breast and the side of the perfect hourglass body. Pulling my clothes off but before stepping out of my boxer briefs, I head over and open the glass door.

"Willa," a deep growl bellows out as she has one of her hands between her legs, fondling herself, with her other hand massaging her left breast. Her neck is bent back like she's enjoying herself too much. Jesus, this is the first time I am really able to take her beauty in all together. The truck did not give much viewing pleasure. She finally brings her head down and locks her eyes on me, chest breathing heavy, letting a moan escape her lips. Slipping out of my briefs, I quickly walk into the shower, grabbing her wrist and pinning it above her head. k

"Baby, I will be the only one making you come. Understand?"

"Yes, Sir," she says as I swipe my fingers between her wet folds and suck them in my mouth, then move her to sit on the shower bench. She is eye level with my cock, and I watch her lick her lips.

"Do you want this, Willa?" I ask as I stroke myself in front of her, my dick already weeping for her. She nods her head yes, placing her hand around me. "Take me, Willa, take all of me." She first uses her tongue to lick from base to tip, before wrapping those sultry pink lips around me.

A deep groan escapes me when she sucks and moves her mouth back and forth, while twirling her tongue around me like a damn popsicle. I have never felt anything so sublime. "Good, Willa. That's a good girl." Placing one hand on the tile in front of me to hold myself up from caving to her touch, I wrap her hair around my other hand as my control to guide her. She doesn't need it because she already knows how to unravel me, lighting the fire within and burning me from the inside out with fevered passion. I know she likes the roughness as she moans around my cock, and that sends a vibration throughout, my knees almost giving in. "Cherry..... You feel...so .... Fucking good.... Cherry...right there...right.... There." I moan as I feel the tip slam to the back of her throat. "Willa, I am about to.... Cherry." Tightening my hair in my hand, she moans again, pushing me to release myself down her throat. She sucks and massages, before pulling back then licking the tip.

"Fuck, Willa. I never....I never have come undone that fast." Keeping a tight grip on her hair, I pull her up to take her mouth with mine.

"I keep craving you and enjoying your engorged length."

Grinning, I hold her tighter. "That is why I have been trying to take it slow with you. Knowing what I want to do to you, knowing I could hurt you."

She whispers, "More," into my mouth, and all self control is gone.

Chapter 16: Breakfast

I look over at the clock, and it says 7:45. Knowing we need to get ready for breakfast, I am not sure I want to leave this blissful spot. Which is me wrapped in Nash's arms as he strokes my arm with his fingertips. Every once in a while, he kisses the top of my head followed by a tight squeeze that pulls us closer together. From the shower to the whirlwind that happened in my bedroom was beyond ecstasy.

Only when I close my eyes can I picture small snippets.

He carries me to my bed and gently lays me down as he stands back up, and I have the best view of this tall, greek god, chiseled specimen where everything about him is vast. Nash stands there, eyeing every inch of my body. Something that has always made me feel self conscious, especially with my scars, but he somehow makes me feel attractive. It is when he notices the long scar up my thigh, he

"Honeysuckle vines," he whispers and kisses it from top to bottom. I lay there speechless, just taking his broadness in and shocked with his gentleness toward me.

"Beautiful Cherry." He continues to kiss me down my leg until he reaches my ankle where another surgery scar is located. He licks the scar, then kisses it. "Your body tells this intense aesthetically vivid story, Willa. These are a part of you, your story. Never feel ashamed," he says as he comes back up, devouring my mouth.

Touching my lips with my fingers, I relive the sensation. Letting out a dreamy sigh, I open my eyes to make sure he is still with me. That this is not all a dream. He kisses the top of my head followed by a tight squeeze, so I close my eyes again.

This time, honing in the exact instant he slid inside my wet center, separating my tight flesh. Taking his time, feeling me stretch as he pushed onward. The groan that escaped him was deep and pleasurable. Asking me to relax, take deep breaths, and to keep looking in his eyes. Telling me I'm such a good girl had me swooning. Never in my life did I think I would be submitting to someone else's desires, but I am finding with him, they are my desires also. Those honey whiskey swirly eyes I get lost in.

My mind drifts back.

My hands come to the sides of his abdomen, wanting to wrap around him, but I remember he tensed to my touch, as I felt his own scars up his side. He swiftly takes my right hand and pins it above my head and interlocks his fingers with mine. Slamming into me harder, my back arches off the bed as I revel in the serene pleasure he is giving me. His salacious mouth coating every inch of me. That damn mouth that comes down to my nipples, his tongue circling around then sucking as he palms the other breast. He fills me with root to tip when we find our slowing rhythm. The moment when you so desperately want to enjoy each other, but soon builds up to a faster pace as the need, the want, the desire to combust takes over. Right when I am nearing the edge, he pulls out just enough so I still feel the tip of him inside of me, leaving me pleading for more.

"Oh, Cherry, I will give you more." Slowly, he pushes back through my center as if we are starting all over again, leaving my body pulsing for him as he again grinds against me. "Fucking hell, Willa. I will never be the same after this." At the time I was lost in my own exhilaration, but now I wonder what the words actually mean. His unrelenting pace with his hardness wrapped tight within me builds the ache in my core.

"Oh, my."

"Willa...... fuck," he groans. "Willa."

"Nash.... Nash!" I scream out, pulling him closer to me as I tighten my fingers in his dark locks to the point of ripping them out. My hips tilt up toward him as I feel the rushing heat escape me, while my muscles clench around him. I ride the tidal wave of the orgasm while he thrusts harder into me, until I feel his whole body tense in satisfaction. My inner workings are still contracting as if they need to milk him for all that he has.

"That's right, Cherry. Take everything you need," he groans while his strained muscles slowly push a few more times to drag out the pleasure. Nash pulls my body closer to him and kisses up my collarbone and neck, whispering, "Never the same again."

Distracting me from my thoughts, Nash says, "Willa, I have no words for what just transpired between us. Describing it would only lessen the moment."

"I agree." Looking back up at him, he bends his head down, kissing me sweetly on the lips.

"My cherry," he whispers against my mouth. "I am not sure how I held back for so long, let alone held myself back in the moment."

"That was you holding back?" I ask with a surprised laugh, thinking how sore my sensitive area is and stretched I feel on the inside. He rolls me over on my back and hovers over me, trailing his finger down my neck, between my breasts, and down to my navel.

"Only half, baby. But I am easing you into this with me because I care about you, and do not want to hurt you."

"I did say 'more.'"

"I promise, there is much more on how I will pleasure you."

Pulling his mouth to mine, I whisper against his lips, "I look forward to it." More pleasurable kissing. "But we should get ready for breakfast and prepare for battle."

"Believe me, I am nothing but prepared to keep what is mine," Nash tells me as he gets out of bed. With his back to me, sliding on his shirt, I see a few scars, but notice they lead over and down his right side, which is furthest from my view. I decide to *save my questions for later. He is so adamant about adoring mine, he needs to let me do the same.*

~~~

We are about to walk inside the breakfast hall of the ranch, and her hand is wrapped in mine. I won't lie saying I am not nervous because the thought of losing her before this morning was an inconceivable notion. Now, my heart seeks it as a death sentence. How on earth can we feel this connected already? Pulling her hand back a little, signaling her to stop, she turns to me. "I have a confession to make before we walk in there."

"Nash, not another one?"

"Do not be mad at your brother, but I sort of talked it out of him this morning about your accident. He made it too easy, and I have been wanting to know. You have been so closed off about it and even riding in general. It just seemed odd to me. I am sorry."

Shaking her head at me, she grumbles, "I am going to kick Dirks' ass later, but for now, thank you for letting me know. And yes, I hate talking about it because it makes me face the nightmare I was a victim of."

"What do they tell you?" I question as I rub my hands down her arms, reassuring her she can tell me anything.

"That I am not cut out for it. Not that I am not fucking fantastic at what I do, because I know I am. More like, there is some type of divine intervention by the devil himself that is out to break me. Everytime I get close to my goal, something tragic happens. My life has been like that since Brooks entered my orbit. And maybe because I see him as a bad omen, it is like I was cursed the day I let him in my life. And me not talking to you about it is because we are new, though I feel like I have known you my whole life. I warned you this ole heart has been battered and bruised. It still really hurts.... All of it. Let alone, how does any of this fit inside your world? The last thing I want to do is embarrass you or your family by being a nobody."

I pull her hard to my chest, wanting to kill the son of a bitch myself. "You are not a nobody, Willa," I say vehemently as I squeeze her tightly against me then push her a little so I can lift her chin up to look at me, my thumbs wiping away her tears. *What did that bastard or anyone else do to her to think she is nothing?*

All this reminds me to check in with Grant on the whereabouts of Brooks. "You are a magnificent work of art. There is no way anyone would think differently or I will personally kick their ass. You ask how all this fits in my world? Because Willa, not sure if you have noticed, but you have quickly become my world. I know I owe you an explanation of my past and scars, and we will discuss it soon, I promise, but know you are worth whatever I could lose along the way in this life. I am realizing it brought me to you, and I plan on keeping you next to me. The feeling of knowing each other since forever is shared. Trust me. I freak myself out daily on how strong my feelings are and what to do with them."

Kissing me, she smiles against my lips. "Don't hold back on me, Cowboy." I pick her up in my arms and swing her around, while kissing her. Until we are interrupted by a throat clearing and a sharp, "Willa."

She jumps out of my arms and straightens her back and clothes. "Good morning, Mama, good morning, Pa."

"Good Morning, Willa. Starting breakfast a little early?" her mom asks and then winks at me.

"Mama, Pa, this is Nash. The guy I was telling you about over dinner the other night."

Her pa speaks up, eying me up and down, "I know exactly who he is."

Holding my hand out to shake, I hold back a grimace. "Sure is a pleasure to meet you, sir."

Bypassing my hand, he continues to walk on by. "Come on, let's grab some breakfast and chat."

Shifting my eyes to Willa as to what the hell just happened, she shrugs her shoulders. Her mom turns and smiles at us and follows behind her husband. I rub my hand over my face then back through my hair. Looking down at Fletcher who seems to be worried as well, I take a deep breath and trail in.

Buffet style, I follow Willa around like a puppy so as to not lose her, and because I am not sitting at the table with her pa by myself. He scares this shit out of me, and I think back to what Clint said about his grandfather being a scary crazy bastard. I try to take in the surroundings to get my nerves in check. Fletcher has his nose in the back of my knee as if I am going down any moment. The walls are covered in cowboy art as well as rawhides and animals. From the ceiling, there are 2 antler chandeliers that hang up over the rustic farmhouse tables, and there are at least ten of them lined throughout the large space.

"Hey. Want me to make a small plate for Fletcher?"

"Um, sure, if it is okay?"

"Breath, Nash. It will be fine."

"Sure, yes, I am fine. I got this."

"Have you ever met a girl's parents before?"

"Not in the sense where my entire happiness is in their hands, no. No, Willa, I have not. Besides, I only had one girlfriend back in high school. No one else has mattered since then."

"Good to know and a lot of information you just released. Taking notes, Cowboy." This gets me to chuckle and relax a bit as we head to the far end table to sit with her family.

"Willa, sit that boy across from me. I want to see him clearly as we speak," her pa says. We take our seats, and I begin to shovel food in my mouth to keep from speaking. Willa leans down and introduces Fletcher to everyone and lets everyone know he is my support dog. Everyone nods, and it goes quiet for a few minutes as everyone begins to eat. This time it is Willa who places her hand on my thigh and squeezes, letting me know all is going to be alright.

Chapter 17: Memory

"Now, son," my pa says to Nash, and I begin to grow nervous about the conversations that are about to be discussed. Our hands are intertwined with slight squeezes between us to calm both of us down.

"We know the past of my parents and your grandparents, Mister Holdings. I am not one to fight feuds of others, but I will fight for my own family and this damn land. So let me tell you straight, there will be no drilling on this land, as long as I am alive. What Willa and Dirks decide after I am six feet under, is on them." Nash nods his head in agreement. "Now that is cleared, I want to know what the two of you know, since I clearly could see the mission on my girl's face and her whispering with her mother."

Mama and I both shyly smile. I tell her everything and sent her a quick text as we headed home last night, asking about the Holdings family and their relation to us. This leads Nash and I to tell my parents about last night and meeting Rosa. How she told us the story and what she said about Nash's grandmother, Lainey, wanting us to be together. My parents nod in understanding, and then my mama pulls out a leather bound journal and pulls a few pictures out of it.

"Willa, this journal was your grandma's, and I want you to have it, read through it. But I also would like to admit we know Rosa also. Your dad grew up with her family and yours, Nash, until the fallout. I know Rosa and Lainey remained closer, but Rosa still kept in touch with Ellie, especially in the last several years prior to Ellie's passing. I think Rosa always wanted to mend the relationship between them all. Not wanting to lose Rosa as a friend also, they would meet up from time to time and even had playdates with their grandkids at the parks. It seems it was not just their kids. Rosa always had the Holdings boys with her too."

Mama slides a picture over to Nash and me. "This is the first picture I found of the two of you."

Gasping, I pick up the picture to look at it closer. I know that it is definitely me because of my red hair, but I have on that light blue shirt that matches my eyes that I always wore. Must be about six, and I am climbing one of those rope ladders. Behind me with his hands on my hips, steadying me and as if to catch me, is a tall, cute boy with some freckles across his cheeks.

He whispers, "Ice blue."

"What?"

"Ice blue. The color of your eyes and what you told me was the color of your shirt. I was not kidding when I told you ice blue has always been my favorite color. I just could not remember why."

We both look at each in astonishment and back at my parents. Sliding another picture over, it is one of me sitting at a table, looking to be part of some fancy tea party.

Nash takes a deeper look. "That is my grandmother's tea set. She used to always host these fancy tea parties and make my brothers and I waiters. We hated these events."

"Look closer," my mama says. We do, bumping our heads together and then laughing. I let him take it first. He shakes his head and passes it over to me. Taking a look, I am stunned to see Nash in the background, staring at me. At least that is what I think he is doing, but he looks mad.

"Why do you look so pissed?"

"Willa!" my mama shrieks.

"Sorry mama, but he does."

"I am thirteen in this picture. You are eleven I guess." I nod, thinking that sounds about right. "Clint is the same age as you. He would not shut up about this beautiful redhead in the tea room. Swearing we knew who you were. So I walked out in the room to deliver drinks when my eyes caught yours, and I dropped the tray. As embarrassed as I was, I could not look away. You can see Clint behind me, giving me hell. I remember that day so vividly now. Later on, I found you outside, trying out Clint's skateboard that he somehow talked you into trying. You had fallen, skinning your knee and hand. I ripped him a new one, sending him to get the first aid kit. You were trying so hard not to cry, so I just sat there and held you until he came back, and I cleaned you up, placing a bandage on your knee."

I am speechless at this moment as mama hands me another picture. It is from the back of us, but Nash has his arm around my shoulders and me leaning against him. Sure enough, we have been part of each other's past. "Thinking back, I went home and wrote in my diary about how cute you were and how you took care of me. Mama, what happened? We never saw each other again?"

"Not really, at least not where it was captured. You all had plenty of play dates together when younger. The next time I was aware you two saw each other was when Nash was a Junior and you were a Freshman. Your high schools played each in football, and if I remember correctly, Nash you were the quarterback."

"Yes, yes I was, ma'am."

"Willa, you were part of the halftime show with your trick riding. All the families were there, and we sat on opposite sides of the fields, but we were all aware of each other's presence. It was post game when most people had left. Willa was waiting for traffic to clear before loading her horse in the trailer. I was walking behind her with her gear, when you came to the parking lot, Nash. You two walked right past each other, but with a quick glance, you both continued walking. I watched as Nash turned back around as if to say something and watched you walk away, Willa. You just shook your head and caught up with your group and that was it. That was the last time I witnessed the two of you near each other. Can't say there have not been other instances, but none that I have witnessed."

"So, Rosa stated Lainey wanted us to end up together. Was Grandma Ellie part of it as well?"

"She was. She had forgiven Lainey a long time before she had passed, but she could not bring herself to be around her, let alone Jacob. I don't think she was ever ready to welcome them back into their lives. From afar, she watched the Holdings boys grow up and knew they had the characteristics, soul, and love of Lainey. None of Jacob. Rosa pretty much was the master at work, keeping tabs on the both of you and sharing details. They are all written in this journal. I am sure your grandmother has one as well, Nash."

"Not complaining, but why Nash? Clint and I are the same age."

"From what Rosa has told me, Nash took to you right away. Clint was on an adventurous path, and Blake was just a toddler. You two played well together, and he was always making sure you were looked after."

I am literally speechless of the odds, trying so hard to relive these memories laid out in front of me. My childhood was so long ago, but Nash seems to recall them quite well now that we are looking at photographs.

Pa speaks up, "There is more. This might be a hard one to swallow. Willa's grandpa was a Major in the Army and had lots of connections. When Lainey found out you were enrolling in the army, she reached out to Henry to ensure your protection. I am not sure he ever got over the fact that I never followed in his shoes and joined the army myself, but he took great pride in you joining the ranks. Behind the scenes, you became his mission to help and protect. Priority and selective missions, before he passed he told me what he had done to protect you for so long, but you had proven yourself of great worth, and it was out of his hands on upcoming missions you were being sent on. Now, I don't know any of the details, but I did read the newspaper when you came home, and judging by your sidekick, it was not pleasant. Henry was honored to watch you become a man and serve your country, so he wanted to make sure I knew to keep tabs on you and be there for your family in any outcome that brought you home. It seems our families have been entwined for a couple of generations now. And I will reiterate, I do not care for past feuds, but as your mama read me some of these journal entries, it was obvious there was a lot of love between your two grandmas, like kindred spirits of some sort. Even apart, they still managed to bring the two of you together it seems, with the help of Rosa. I know this is a lot to take in, but before we move onward, I have a few other things I would like to ask you, son."

I turn to Nash who still seems to be absorbing what my pa just spewed out, along with bracing himself to what is to come. Fletcher is halfway in Nash's lap at this point, and I am on the edge of my seat with what is about to come.

Nash nods to my pa, who proceeds. "Now, Nash, all past aside, all oil aside. Do you see my daughter as part of your future?"

"Yes, sir. I do."

"Are your intentions pure with her? As in no oil deals, no shared personality of your late grandfather, no use and then leave?"

"I only want Willa to be happy, and I will do whatever that takes. Also, I do not share my grandfather's idealized conceptions of family and friends with business. Neither do my brothers or parents."

"Good. Now do you support this rodeo lifestyle she lives? Yes, she is also a teacher, but her first love has always been the rodeo. How do you plan on supporting her?"

"I absolutely support her, and from the little I have seen, she is a force. I will support her in whatever way she needs me too. Whether that is standing next to her, in the stands, sponsoring her, or being there to hold her. You have my word, sir."

Pa puts his hand out. "It is nice to finally meet you, son. I look forward to getting to know you more."

"Thank you, sir. Me too," Nash chokes out, shaking Pa's hand, allowing me to breathe a little easier.

Chapter 18: Always

After an informative breakfast, we are back in my cabin with awkward silence. Not sure where and what we do next; the only thing I do know for sure is I need to go for a run and practice with Ringo. Leaving Nash on the couch, I head to my room to change, only to come back and notice he has not moved.

"Hey, I am heading out for a run and then practice. Feel free to hang out."

"Run, that's a good idea. I think I need to head back to my apartment. My parents are back in town, and I need to work on some things."

"Okaayy..... Yeah, just call me later." Nash comes over and kisses me on the forehead then walks out with Fletcher hot on his heels. After a few minutes of me just standing there like a dumbfounded buffoon, I groan in frustration. *He just fuckin' left. What the actual hell?"*

I walk out on my front porch, popping my headphones in and stretching my legs. Looking up, I see Nash sitting in his truck, staring at me. If he wants to talk, he knows where to find me. Because I have no idea what is going on that handsome head of his nor does he want to share. So placing my shades on, I take off running down my usual path, blaring music in my ears to tune out all else.

~~~~

Frozen in the truck, not able to think straight or move. It is not like any of the news was earth shattering, but enough to make me look over my childhood and past with a different lens. Willa just walked out on her porch, and I have a good sense she is not happy with me. I'm such an asshole just leaving her here with not much to go on. The scary glare I am receiving back through my windshield is not promising, but before I can think of what to do, she takes off running. Just as I am about to chuck my phone across the truck because I have the urge to break something, it rings. It's Clint.

"Hey, brother."

"Hi."

"How did breakfast go?"

"It was fine. Now Willa is pissed at me."

"Bro, what did you do?"

"Honestly…. fuck. … I completely shut down on her."

"Start from the beginning."

So I do, filling him in on all this family nonsense, photographs, the feeling of being impaired to the point of not being able to process anything, and that I felt I was just approved by her pa to marry her.

"Damn, bro. There is a lot to impact there, so let me break it down. Past is past, and it seems her side of the family is willing to move on. You need to break the news to Dad, Holdings will no longer be pursuing the

Crenshaw land then share the news of Willa with both parents. That's if she does not leave your ass."

"Agree."

"Looking at the pictures, and thinking about your encounters with Willa, has it not clicked that she has always been the one? The reason why you only had one girlfriend who was the complete opposite of Willa in looks and personality. Why no other woman makes it past a one night stand with you? Come on, man!"

"Shit, Clint. Hearing her mom earlier, it made everything so clear on why we seem so connected. My draw to her. Then her dad mentioned the Army, and my mind went back to all the missions and the one that sent me home." Tears are welling up, and I'm not sure I am in a place to control my emotions anymore.

"Willa deserves someone who is not broken. Someone strong. Not who leads his soldiers to death, who fights mentally to live every day because I should have died with them or instead of them. I can't put her through this."

"Brother, you listen to me and get out of your fucking head. You are not responsible for those deaths, those terrorists are. Those that created the mission have that blood on their hands, not you. You deserve to live just as much as any of them. You want to screw this up with Willa, be my guest, but if you feel shitty about your life right now, I can only imagine how you are going to feel once she is gone. This whole week has been a whirlwind of crazy shit, but you have been my old brother again and happy. And dammit, I am going to be selfish. I need you to be selfish and not fuck this up and live your life. I know you were close to them, and I cannot imagine the messed up shit you saw on your tours, but they would not want you mourning their lives year after year without moving on. You went through your own horrors and shit. You paid your dues."

"I get it. I am just tired of putting up this front, and you're right. I have been more of myself in the past week than I have in the last several years."

"You have to let the choice be hers, brother. You cannot make this decision for her, or you will break her heart, and there will be no taking you back. And from what you have told me. she has been through her fair share of shit also. So take all the damn signs, call it fate, whatever and just man up and tell her."

"I see her running down the hill now. Let me talk to her, and I'll see you later at dinner."

"Good luck, bro."

CHAPTER 19: HARD

Willa slows down as she reaches my truck, and I step out.

"I thought you had things to do? Here I was taking the long way around to make sure you were gone before I got back."

"Fair enough. Can we go talk? I need to explain some things to you. If you need me to leave after, I will."

"Sure, come on in." Letting Fletcher out of the truck, we follow her in.

Willa has already distanced herself to the other side of the room, but I need to be close to her. Walking over, she tenses.

"Please do not think I am going to hurt you."

"I don't. Just after this morning and the conversations we had, you just turned into a fuckin' frozen pickle."

Trying to contain my chuckle at her choice of words, I blurt out, "I know, and I am sorry. So sorry, Willa. This morning was overwhelming to say the least. Your dad brought up the whole army thing….I…I…I was triggered. Literally have been on the phone with Clint since you left to have him talk me off the ledge of leaving you."

Her eyes go wide, and I know I need to back track fast, but I know I am not mentally or emotionally in the place to handle any of this right. Judging by the look on her face, I am foreignn territory now.

"Ugh, I am so fuckstrated! This is not something I need right now."

"There is that damn word again! What the hell do you mean by that?"

"It means I don't like feeling like this. Helpless, confused, on the verge of being broken. The need to beg, but my pride refuses to let you see me fall. You make me feel like such a damn girl, and I hate it. Damnit, Nash. I am not going to play the game of you coming or going, having that single thought always sitting in the back of mind that you are going to have to be talked off a cliff of leaving me. Ever heard the term, heart like a truck?" Nodding my head no, she continues, "It means it has been dragged through the mud, beaten up with the dents and scratches to show for it. That my heart is willing to be put in drive to ride with you down whatever highway or backroad we find ourselves on as long as you care for me in all the ways I need and want. But shit, Nash, after this whirlwind of a week, chemistry that could spark Hades flame to only get whiplash by your emotions is too much right now. I have two weeks to get my ass in gear to start qualifying for the American. If you cannot be next to me then I just need you to leave. Today was a lot, I get that. I also know you have your own demons you are fighting, so please go fight them, and then maybe, you will be willing to share with me on what makes you tick. Why you cringe when I touch your side, why you are such a dominant not just in the bedroom but in life, or the vacant look I see in those brown eyes of yours when you think I'm not look'n."

"Willa, come on. Let's talk through this."

"No, Nash. I can't. Not right now. I need time. This is me being selfish for my own peace of mind and to focus on my goals. Neither one of us expected any of this, so this is the perfect time to digest it all while we figure out our next move."

"My move is to be with you, Willa." Moving closer to her, I place my hands on her shoulders.

"Nash," she whispers while hitting her forehead on my chest. "I need you to go. Please.....please don't make me beg."

"Know that I am not going to stop wanting to be with you. No matter how much time you need."

"I really hope not, but it is not just me that needs the time, Cowboy. You need to figure out *you*. So please go."

All I can do at this point is nod my head in agreement because I screwed this up. Her eyes are filling with water, and I know she is trying so hard not to break down in front of me. That pride she mentioned, keeping her from falling into my arms, to let me hold and comfort her. I pull her in for a hug, kissing the top of head and taking in her honey vanilla scent one more time. Turning around, I take a deep breath before walking out the door. I lean against the front door for a few minutes. Long enough to hear her body slam against the wooden door then slide down as Willa breaks down. With each sob I hear, my heart cracks a little more. Finding my willpower to not rush in there, to pick her up and hold her, is hard because as much as I despise these unraveling events right now, she is right. I need to fight these demons to move on.

Not sure I am going to get through dinner with my family as my body feels cold and numb without her next to me. My soul is pleading to not become the self-aversion person I was before her. My heart fills my chest with excruciating pain. Finding myself unable to breathe, I rush to my truck, punching the steering wheel, then burying my face in my hands in frustration and tears. I will give her time, us time, because one thing I know for certain is, it has always been her.

~~~

With the door being the only thing holding me half up, I lose myself in emotion, not able to think of the last time I cried this hard. When have crocodile tears streamed down my face in a rush? *Fuck, never have I ever. Not until now, not until Nash.* Not through being abused, losing a title I had in my grasp, the injuries, almost losing my horse, and anything and everything in between has not broken me like he has. As if a piece of me was put back in place, only to be taken away and shredded. The feeling of emptiness is unbearable as I curl up the floor, alone and cold.

Chapter 20: Rodeo

It has been two weeks since Nash walked out of my cabin. I won't say my life because he still makes his presence known. Nash texts me every morning, afternoon, and at bedtime. Though it took several days for me to be in a place to respond back, I finally broke down and did. Now we chat through text like the beginning, getting to know each other a little more.

With this, he has started to open up. He sends me daily emails including snippets of his life. Childhood memories that we seemed to have shared along with memories of his life. It only took me a few emails to realize they are being sent in chronological order. I believe it is only time until I receive one about his time in the army. At least I hope so because that would mean he really is opening up in a deeper sense. That he is allowing himself to be vulnerable. Dealing with his demons that I know in my heart are brought on by his whole conscience and not because he is actually responsible for what happened in that damn country, years ago.

Pa had filled me in on what had happened overseas with the mission. He saw me broken, and I could tell it was breaking my hard-ass of a dad, when he pulled me into a bear hug, and all I could do was cry, "Oh, Pa, I miss him," as I snotted and cried all over his overalls as he held me, trying to calm his little girl through the storm, that he is not sure how to handle. One thing, if it would be one of the few guys that have been around; I would receive the lecture of cowgirls don't cry, Willa. He ain't worth the dirt under your feet.

Or if it was Brooks when I only cried in pain, not because I felt emotionally splintered. Pa wanted to kill him, and the only time in my entire life that it was okay to cry. I remember just looking at him in bewilderment, blinking my eyes, trying to force tears out. I thought it would make him believe I was less fragile if I let some tears out, instead of the silence that had dragged on for days after the attack.

Knowing the history of Nash and me, seems to have his thoughts in knots. A week after my hostile takeover I kept unleashing at the ranch—at least I kept most of my shit together at school—Pa sat me down to fill in the gaps of the mysterious Nash.

Now it's Wednesday, and I am with Tilly and Amity. We are loaded up with Ringo and Tilly's horse, Ace, heading to Fort Worth for the rodeo. We are borrowing a badass truck and horse trailer with sleeping quarters for the weekend that Amity said she borrowed from an unnamed friend. I am just too excited to even pry her for more information. Just thankful for the nice ride and sleeping accommodations for the rest of the week. With Amity driving, I am able to study the competition and get in the event headspace I need. It has also been ruled it is a no guy, no Nash weekend. No one is allowed to ask about us or him. I have been pretty hush about what has been going on with us. They just know we are taking time to figure out ourselves and not really together at the moment.

Four hours later, we finally made it to the arena and checked in. I take Ringo in to walk him around the arena to help him get his bearings. We start with roping tomorrow and qualify for timed trials. It has already been a long day so I know we are all going to crash hard later this evening. Luckily for us, our trailer is close to the holding area for the horses. I have Ringo as close to the end and on the outside as I could get it. So looking out the trailer window, I can at least see him and definitely hear him when he has lots to say to the fellow horses surrounding him.

The girls and I close out the evening catching up with fellow riders, throwing back a few beers and reminiscing of old times and catching up on the new.

~~~

It is midday on Thursday, and I have Blake feeding me all the information on Willa. Since Paramour, he and Amity have been taken with each other, so much so he let her borrow his brand new truck, *that I am not entirely sure he did not purchase to impress the cowgirl herself,* and rented a state of the art horse trailer for them to borrow under the radar. Not only did he do it because he is trying to impress the girl, but to ensure Willa's safety and spoil her a bit since I am not allowed to. We only talk through texts, and she never responds to any message about feelings. Blake is fully aware of what has been going on with Willa and me. With this knowledge, he has literally been in my office since seven this morning giving me the play by play of the day from Amity. I owe them both a nice luxurious weekend away. According to Amity, Willa and Ringo have been kicking ass all morning in team roping and sitting and holding at number three with qualifying.

By two in the afternoon, Willa and Tilly were first in team roping, Willa was sitting second in calf roping and was pushed back to fourth in qualifying for barrel racing. Of course, we have been watching the videos Amity has been sending, and I cannot believe what a savage my girl is when she enters the arena. Every inch of me wants to hold her and be there with her, but I am respecting the boundaries she has laid out. Plus, I know she does not need the added distraction of my presence there.

Clint pointed out that she will probably be pissed when she finds out Amity is spoon feeding me information. In my defense, Amity is one of her best friends. I could have easily sent Grant to spy on her. I continue to click through emails as Blake walks out to take a call, and Clint strolls back in.

"Hey, Bro."

"Hey. Need something?"

"Yeah. You thought anymore about what Dad said at dinner that night?"

"No. Not really. My priority right now is not to piss her off again and get her back. Dad has a great idea, but I made promises, and right now, I just need everyone to respect that while I take time to figure it out."

"I get it, man. I really do. Well those guys are in Montana right now and will be heading this way in a month. Just giving you a timeline because that is my job."

"I know."

"Are you two even truly not together?"

"I do not even know. I have not heard her voice in about two weeks. She answers my texts, and I know she is reading my emails. I have been going to the Veteran PTSD meetings three times a week, and I really think they have been helping and just knowing I am not alone in this. So many other men and women are going through similar shit." Looking down at Fletcher at my feet, I murmur, "I would say he has enjoyed the reprieve from my nightmares lessening, but he has to deal with my daily angst over Willa." He looks up at me as soon as I say her name, letting me know he misses her too. Clint chuckles because he knows what a horrid mess I have been these past weeks around the office, to the point where everyone takes extra measures to stay out of my way.

Blake comes back in and takes a seat in the chair he has been in all day. He begins tapping his foot on the ground, so both Clint and I look over at him.

"What has your balls wound so tight?" Clint jokes.

"Nothing." But as the pallor on his face turns white, I know not to believe him.

"Fuck, bro. What was that call about? Just say it."

He takes a minute, looks down at his phone like he is debating a choice he thinks he has. Clint quickly reaches for the phone, grabbing it then looks at the screen. "Who is this?" Blake doesn't answer, so Clint slides the phone across my desk. It is a grainy photo at best, but I can tell it is a guy standing next to a latched gate.

"Blake, who is this?"

"Amity sent me the pic. That guy is at the rodeo this weekend."

"Don't make me hold you down and waterboard your ass. Can you please speak like you have something to say?" I threaten because the longer I stare at this picture and soak in Blake's words, goosebumps rise over my body as if a bucket of ice was thrown over me.

"Fuck, she might kill me, but you need to know. Amity called to chat, and she all the sudden seemed taken back, as she gasped. I asked her what was wrong, and she said Willa's ex was there. Amity seemed genuinely scared on the phone, so I made her explain to me why an ex is such a big deal. I stayed on the phone with her while she told Willa. Willa said just to ignore him. Not pay any attention to him because he is not allowed near her anyways. That she could handle him if needed. Man, I am sorry. Surely that fucker wouldn't try anything stupid in such a public setting, right?"

I feel the weight of Fletcher on my lap, there is a loud ringing in my ear as I clench my fists while only seeing red. I hear Clint tell Blake to get the jet ready for Fort Worth. I sense Clint behind me before I feel his hands on my shoulders, shaking me slightly to get me to tap back in. I do after what seems like forever, but not even a full minute.

"Bro, you are going to explain everything to me so I know how to clean up this mess once done, but we have a flight to catch first."

Chapter 21: Control

  What a day. What a flippin' horse hair of a day. It started off great, but I won't lie, the news that Brooks is here really put a damper on my mood. The whole damn experience for that matter. I have no idea who Amity was talking to when she came over to show me the picture of him from the other side of the arena, letting Tilly and I know about him. Which has made me want to do some bestfriend prying, because she has been either texting or talking on her phone since we got here. To the issue at hand, I don't doubt for a second Brooks knows I am here, but for the life of me, I can't imagine what he is doing here. He doesn't ride, and it was never really his kind of scene to partake in. I know he hated that I was part of it and took time from him.

The arena is getting set up for the bull riding tonight, and I am more than ready to take a shower then relax and watch. The girls and I first were able to pull over an extra guard to watch our horses in the paddock because there is no way I trust Brooks

He may have to stay away from me, but what is stopping him from doing something stupid or dangerous where I'm concerened? I might have been naive a few years ago, but dammit if I don't know now, narcissistic abusive assholes never change. Leaving the girls at the paddocks, I head back into the arena to the locker room showers.

Arms are all the sudden wrapped around me, squeezing me tight as I feel hot breath at the base of my neck. I don't recognize the smell. and I am too frozen in fear to look anywhere but straight ahead.

"Is that how you treat an old friend?" The voice is low and hoarse. The arms slowly release me to turn me around. Looking up, I am ready to slap the hell out of him.

Grabbing my wrist, he stops me mid-strike. "Damn, Willa Bee, I forgot just how fiesty you are."

"Damnit, Luke! You can't just be running around here and grabbing people from behind. You're lucky the back of my heel didn't meet your nutsack tonight." I growl, glaring at him.

"My apologies, Willa. I forgot your history. I was just so excited to see you on the lineup and out there doin' your thing today."

"Thanks, Luke. It's fine. I take it you are riding tonight. Who did you draw?"

"That damn giant bastard, Spook." My eyes go wide because I know exactly who he just mentioned. That bull has some of the longest horns I have seen on a rodeo bull, and he takes no prisoners. If you fall off of Spook, you better be quick to get up before he stomps all of you, or worse, throws you across the dirt.

"Good luck with that one tonight. The girls and I will be in the stands cheering you on. Oh by the way.... Since you are here, do you have my horse trailer by any chance?"

"Ah shit, Willa, look at the time. I gotta go. We can catch up later." He kisses my cheek before sprinting away.

"Damn you, Luke. I'm going to track your ass down! You can't charm your way out of this!" I shout out to him.

Muttering to myself that I am going to literally kick his ass, I walk to the locker room, knowing damn well he could charm himself out of any situation. Even could sell fire to a dragon. I drop my bag on the bench, pull out my shower stuff, and lay my clothes out, all while noticing there are at least 4 other people in here right now. I do enjoy the fact that there are shower stalls here, unlike the guys locker room is just wide open.

Relaxation finally hits me as I lean against the wall, letting the water pour over me. With so many big wins today, I feel relieved that maybe now is finally my time to win this. Sure, I have a long way to go, but Ringo and I are killing it out there. With each pass, we get more attuned with each other and faster. With all of this going on, I wish I could call Nash and share the news. We have not verbally spoken since he left my house that day. Hades, I miss that man. The water turns off next to me, pulling me out of my Nash daydream.

Now it's eerily quiet, too quiet. "Hello," I say loud enough that someone could answer me if they are at least in this back section. Silence is all I get. Looking at my watch, I see the bullriding starts in twenty minutes, so I guess I need to get my ass in gear. Rinsing the conditioner out of my hair and soap off my body, I turn the water off and wrap myself up in my towel.

"Nice of you to finally come out and join me." This time I do not need to even look when I hear the voice that turns my body cold as nails are being driven in. I begin to feel lightheaded, thinking this must be a nightmare.

"Oh come on, sweetheart. You might as well walk all the way out here before I come get you. Make this easy on yourself."

Pushing to get my nerves together, I straighten up and walk out to the locker area to see him sitting next to my bag and thumbing through my phone.

"Why are you here, Brooks?"

"To see you of course."

"You are not allowed near me. You should not be in the room, let alone this building with me in it."

"Oh, sweetheart. Do you really think a piece of paper is going to stop me after all this time?" The flicker in my eyes must tell him everything he needs to know. "You really do. That is cute, Willa. You always had that innocence about you. Cute but annoying at times."

"You need to leave, Brooks."

"I'm here with some friends. Thought I would just come by to say hi, no harm done." As he stands up and walks towards me, he rakes his eyes over my body. "You looked real good out there today." He moves in closer as I start to take steps back. He doesn't stop until my back slams against the lockers, holding on to my towel for dear life. "Now, Willa, you think I really want to hurt you after all this time? Sure, you ruined my life for a few years. Had to move aways from my friends and family, but those are just bygones, right?" Brooks' fingers inch toward my towel, and I feel his touch on my skin, trying to pull the towel off of me.

"Please, just leave me be." My muscles tighten as I use all my strength to hold the towel on my body.

"You can scream, but no one can hear you. You can run, if you can get past the door." He gives me a wink that sends aching chills down my spine. "I think it is past time we reminisce about the good times, don't you think?" His palm rides up my bare leg, inching close to my sex, leaving me shaking. "I am going to need you to calm down, sweetheart, and enjoy what I'm about to give you." Yanking my hair to the right, Brooks moves me from the lockers, then with all his strength, he tosses me to the floor, leaving me scrambling to get my towel back over my body. But he is so much quicker than I am and throws it to the side.

"You are still the best pussy I ever had, Willa. Do you think your new boyfriend will be okay with me taking back what belongs to me?" My expression from bitch changes to fear as much as I wish I could fight it. "I read your texts. I know what you have been up to lately. Tell me, does he know how delicate you are? How easy you bruise?" Growling, he pushes his thumb into a pressure point on my leg that shoots pain up my back and over. I cry in pain. "Don't you start crying, you know how much I despise that."

"Brooks, please just let me go. Go live your life and leave me alone."

SLAP!

"Someone has forgotten her manners. You do not speak unless spoken to."

SLAP!

"Do you remember now?" All I can do is nod as the sting on both my cheeks overwhelms my senses. "Good. Now, sweetheart, we can do this the easy way by you giving in, or you fight me, leaving me no choice but to harm this precious body and face so you remember who I am to you. What's it going to be?"

Gritting through my teeth, I scream, "Fuck you!" Bracing myself for what surely is to come, I'm surprised when it doesn't. I slowly look up, meeting his face of astonishment. SHIT.

"You always had a dirty mouth. I think it's about damn time someone shuts you up for good. But not before I have my way with you." A swift punch to the side of my head causes me to fall back, seeing stars. Everything is swirling around me, but I feel him above my naked body, palming my breast, still talking, but I am unable to make any sense of it. I hear a belt come off then I feel it being wrapped around my wrists and tightened against the bench. Trying to focus, Brooks pulls his dick out of his pants, giving it a few strokes before coming back to hover above me. I find all my strength, letting out the loudest scream I can muster up. That earns me a punch in my sides, not once but twice. I scream again, and he continues to punch my side until I am positive at least one rib is cracked.

"You know I am the best you will ever have, so just lay there and enjoy it, sweetheart."

Right then, I hear banging on the door. Several muffled male and female voices yelling through. I yell back and take my chance, kneeing Brooks in his manhood since he is distracted by the noise from the otherside of the door. He bends over, so I crawl backwards as quickly as I can. *Fuck, I am tied to the bench. I can't go anywhere.*

"You fucking bitch. You will pay for that." With that, he clenches his fist, and it heads straight for my face. I feel it hit, once, twice, three times, then nothing. I hear muffled voices. Only seeing shadows move around me in the darkness. I feel my arms being released then coming back to my body. I feel my body being carried away. Unable to make any shapes, movements, or voices out, I close my eyes completely.

CHAPTER 22: RECOVER

I almost killed that son of a bitch. If Clint and Blake had not pulled me off of him, I would have. Now I am sitting in Willa's hospital room next to her with a broken hand, waiting for her to wake up. I need her to wake the fuck up. The doctors put her in a medically induced coma because of all the swelling. *The sick bastard.* I slowly glide my fingertips down her face where she has a few facial bones broken, a horrific black eye with all this covered in black and purple on her right side. Her left side has slight bruising, but nothing compared to the right. Her body is covered in bruises from top to bottom, and the X-rays also confirmed broken ribs.

When we finally busted through the damn door and saw her knocked out, belted to the bench, my heart clenched so hard, I nearly fell to the ground. Fletcher was ready to pounce if I went down. I remember him barking through the whole chaotic scene. Blake and Clint ran to pull Brooks off of Willa so I could get to her. She just laid there, lifeless. My feisty, full of life, tough as nails girl was broken. Rage surged through me until I was pulled off of him. By then, the paramedics had entered the room. Once I released her from the bench and picked her up, there was no giving her up. I carried her out to the ambulance, then laid her on the stretcher. Never leaving her side. Never letting go of her hand and always kissing it. She squeezed it a few times. All I can do was pray she knows it is me that has her.

~~~

Two days have passed, and I have only left her side to shower. Fletcher lays on her left side, providing the warmth and comfort he knows how. All other matters can wait. Both sets of parents have come by numerous times. Despite what brought them together, it has been nice seeing them catch up and be here for Willa. The last dinner I had with them after I had left Willa's, was as expected. My parents had known all along about us and the history.

Dad agreed to leaving the Crenshaws' land alone, as he only had it on the schedule to push me out that way. He knew we would never run into each other otherwise, so his plan was to get me in front of her and see what I would do. Little did anyone know that fate had different plans, allowing everything to spiral quickly. My mother believes divine intervention always had a plan and was just waiting for the perfect time. Can't say I disagree with her after all that has transpired in just a month.   Clint and Blake state they have work handled so I have not been on my phone except to make sure Brooks is being handled properly and working on getting Willa transferred back to San Antonio as soon as she wakes up and is cleared. The morning rounds doctor stated the swelling has gone down tremendously so they stopped the infusion other than pain meds. That it could be any time now. Willa is the one in control now.

~~~

Day four, I am pulled out of exhaustion with Willa's whines and screams. Her body is shaking and looking as if she is struggling. I can only imagine what her mind is re-playing for her, but I need to get her out of this state. I call in the nurse, and we both work on coaxing her out of the nightmare. After several minutes, her eyes flutter open, and she locks her eyes on me.

"Nash," she hoarsely whispers.

"Don't speak. Let me get you some water."

A few sips get her coughing, so I move in to sit her up more carefully. Her arms go around my neck, pulling me down to her.

"Willa, I don't want to hurt you."

"I don't care. I just need you with me, touching me."

"I am right here. Not going anywhere." I slowly sit up, kissing her on the forehead. She squirms a bit at the touch, then places her hand on her face so she can feel the bandages.

"How bad is it?"

"Some broken facial bones. You had severe brain swelling, so you have been in an induced coma for the last few days. Broken ribs. But nothing that will not heal. The plastic surgeon said he did not see anything that would cause scarring."

"Wow." She blinks her eyes a few times. "I think he planned on killing me."

"Not going to lie to you. A few more punches to the head, and he would have."

"Wait, you came for me? How did you know?"

"Amity told Blake, who told me."

"What?" She stares up at me, looking helpless and clueless.

"Apparently those two are together. Have been since Paramour. They have kept it a secret from you since we were apart, and she knew you had a lot riding on the rodeo."

"Hmmmm, ok. I'll have words with her later. Hades! The rodeo."

"Don't worry about that. Every one bore witness to you when I carried you out of the locker room. Your sponsor has all intentions to cover you in the next event, and everyone is cheering you on. And this time, I will be right by your side."

"Wow, okay. Well at least it won't take this long to heal, and I can hopefully be on the road for next month's show."

"How about we take this one day at a time for right now? First, we need to get you back to San Antonio, then released, then home. Speaking of home, I would really love it if you came home with me to Horseshoe Bay." She nods a yes, which completely throws me back because I expected push back.

"Really? No push back?"

"No. I don't want to be away from you any longer. All I wanted was to call you and share in all the excitement with you. To hear your voice. I know we have things to work through, but I want us to do it together."

"Oh, Cherry, I could not agree more." Pulling her in my arms, I rock her back and forth, vowing to never let her go again.

Chapter 23: Normal

Two and half weeks later, I am finally heading back to my little cabin so I can report back to work. I have missed the ranch, my students, the normalcy of my life. Nash and I sit in the back of his SUV while Grant drives us. A two hour drive has me reflecting on the weeks as Nash attends to a work emergency. He has been putting out fires over the last week due to the time he took off to care for me. I fought him to work. To not tend to me every time I moved or wanted something, but he refused. Even now, he has his palm resting on my thigh, giving it a squeeze every so often. To the point I believe he does it more for his comfort than mine. Turning back to look at him, he gives me a wink that melts my heart in the middle of his tongue lashing to the poor soul on the other end of the line.

For two weeks, I lived in a fancy house, overlooking a lake as large as the ocean from where I stood. The house sat up on the hill a bit from the others, giving a perfect view from any mammoth-sized window on the back of the house, the back deck, or my favorite, his heated infinity pool. Nash has tended to my every want and need. No intimacy other than a few minor makeout sessions. Definitely not for the lack of trying on my part, but he denied me, saying my body was not ready. His concern was also for my mental state. *Huh, my mental state.* Not sure that has ever been classified as normal or intact in medical terms.

Again, my reaction to Brooks' attack left me numb and tearless. I refuse to shed tears over the attack, but no one else sees it that way. I even heard my pa talking to Nash a week ago on the back deck after dinner about my state of mind. I held my tongue because I was in no mood for another argument over my emotions. Bruises have healed, my face looks eighty percent better. Ninety-five percent better when I push through the pain to apply makeup. Which is exactly what I did today because I need to feel like a living human. The need to feel pretty. The need to not have Nash's whiskey eyes look at me in pity anymore.

With all going on, Nash and I have tread around the issues we need to work through. He has continued to send me emails daily so I had more to read then just my "naughty" books as he calls them. I am now caught up to his last year in the army, bracing myself for the email coming. Which is why maybe I did not get one for the past two days. I know this is hard for him, but damn, I need him to let me in.

Blake secretly told me he was attending a veterans PTSD program before the accident. That he has kept in touch with the group virtually since we have been at Nash's house. That information alone made my tears fall. Nash is fighting his demons not just for him, but for us. Solidifying what I mean to him. Yes, we seem to have this crazy connection with a past we were thrown into it seems, but we are so intertwined with each other, it hurts physically to be apart. He gets me on a whole other level than anyone ever has. All my quirks, which are a lot. Nash knows how to break through my tough exterior when I need it the most. Lets me rant when I need to, to be stubborn to an extent and even lies with me in the rain. My missing piece has been given back to me, and I plan on keeping it until the end.

~~~

Grant pulls in to park in front of Willa's cabin. But I can't seem to look away from this precious, alluring woman sitting next to me who has me worried by how quiet she has been on the ride over. Granted, I was on the phone troubleshooting for a good bit of the drive, but she just has a far off look in her eyes. She must be compartmentalizing the month in her head, doing her own troubleshooting and worrying. For me, I know this needs to be the time I lay my cards on the table with her. After all the shit she has gone through, all the time we have spent apart for years.

Willa slides out the door quickly before I can grab her hand. Rushing out behind her, she yelps when I pick her up bridal style to carry her in.

"Nash, seriously."

"Yes, seriously. Indulge me please." She huffs under her little grin. Secretly, she loves me to dote on her. Secretly under her tough, fierce exterior she is a true lover and cuddler. I also know better than to say that to her face because she will try her damndest to beat me up. I chuckle to myself because it is pretty adorable when she tries, only for me to lock her wrists together in one hand and tease her with the other, making her forget why she was irate with me to begin with.

"What is that grin for?" she asks as I put her down on the couch in her living room.

"Just thinking about how I use my handsome looks and charm for good."

"Oh really there, Cowboy." Sitting her on the couch, looking into her icy blue eyes is all I need to push forward.

"Of course. But right now, I need to tuck those away and be serious with you for a few." She nods, as if knowing what I am about to say.

Deep breath in, I stand up. Another deep breath in while pulling my shirt off over my head, I start, "These are the scars I have to remember the day several of my squad were killed. Let alone the dozen other civilians and kids that were murdered. For whatever reason, I was spared and spared as a whole. I had two other men make it, but one lost his legs, and the other lost his arm and body was severely burned. Shards of metal ripped though my muscles and tissues with a broken leg and shoulder. For physical injuries, that was all, while the others lost so much more. For years now, I have not been able to come to terms with any of it and how those lost had so much more to live for. To go home too. I have Fletcher because the first several months I was home, I would hit the ground every time there was a loud noise. High stress moments trigger panic attacks for me, which then make me hallucinate back to the scene. I have been sedated more times than I can recall, and the nightmares are hell."

Willa slowly stands up and walks closer to me, cautiously reaching out to me. Closing the gap between us, she gently glides her fingertips down my side, and I try to hold still as she touches what has been so forbidden to me for so long.

"My need for control for so long, especially during sex has been because I have not wanted others to see me. To touch me and be disgusted like I am. Hands are kept away from my body. Kissing is not allowed. To not be swept up in the moment. Keeping focus and control has been my endgame. Pleasure and get out."

"Nash……" she whispers in a long sigh. "You make so much more sense now. You have told me time and time again to love my scars, the stories they tell. It's time you do the same. I can't begin to relate what hell you went through or losing people in such a circumstance, but I also know, from being around my grandpa, shit happens. Life happens with all its dirty mess. We live in a beautiful but cruel world. The stories he would tell my brother and I and photographs he shared of his time at war was horrific. He was so brave and so are you. You don't have to tell me the story now. Don't be mad, but Blake let it slip that you had joined the Veterans group, which I think is wonderful. Just don't shut me out. If you still have a thought of walking away from us, then just do it now because my heart is like a truck, and you leaving will push it to the salvage yard. There will be no rewiring or gasoline filled dreams left for me."

Bringing my hands to her face to pull her to my lips is satisfaction. "You have always been the only one, Willa. It has only ever been you my heart was searching for." Kissing again, I hoist her up around my waist and head to the couch.

"You coming back in my life a month ago had me feeling more like myself than I had in a long time. I have wanted to wake up, to be alive and be thankful. That is because of you. The thought of losing that because you fear I am not strong enough or handle my moments."

"That is what you are calling them?" She smiles, trying to bring light among the conversation. "Apollo, Nash. Can't you tell that I am madly in love with you. Apparently always have been."

"I love you, Willa. So damn much."

"Make love to me, Nash…..Please."

"I will, baby, but let me taste you first."

We both stand, hurriedly stripping each other of clothes, before I carry her back to her bed. I lay down on the bed and let her straddle me.

"Closer," I growl, "closer. I need to taste you and make you scream first." Dipping my palm past her clit ring, I smear my fingers in her wetness. "You are already so wet for me, Cherry." Not able to hold back any longer, I raise her up by her ass cheeks to set her on my face. Before she can even argue, my tongue swipes up her pink wet folds. She moans, and I watch with my eyes as she places her hands on the headboard. My hands clench her ass, slowly pushing and pulling her over my mouth and tongue as I suck, nibble, and lick at her juiciness. She is fastly coming undone, as I twirl my tongue inside of her, moaning my name. I promised I would make her scream it. Shifting one of my hands to massage her clit while I continue to lap her, my cherry begins to buck against my mouth, and it is an immaculate sight to watch her unravel on top of me. Willa's body shudders out of her orgasim as she shouts my name. My cock now painfully bulging, I flip her down to her back and hover above her. I line myself up at her opening and slowly push in.

"Nash, More!" she yells.

Grunting and groaning, I am trying not to say every explicit word under the sun during this moment. But, "Fuck, you are so tight, Willa. You were made for me. Every part."

Wrapping her legs around my waist so I slide deeper in, she pulls me down to kiss her.
In and out, in and out, as our sweaty skin slaps against each, making the best noise while I ready myself to release inside of her.

"Wait for me, Cherry."

"I'm trying. Please, Nash, fill me up."
Slamming back into her several more times, she is withering beneath me. "Now, Willa. Now." I feel her sex clench around my shaft, milking me for every last drop, her fingernails digging into my back as we stare into each other's eyes. Bodies hyper aware of the other post, the most intense experience of my life. "Good girl, Cherry."

"That was the best make up sex ever," she says exhaustingly.

"Agree," I murmur, kissing her red, swollen lips. Only to begin again.

EPILOGUE

Three months later....

Nerves are taking over my entire being while driving my truck down this old dirt road. The end of this dirt road holds my future with the fiery redhead sitting next to me blindfolded.

"Nash. Oh my Hades, this road is so bumpy. Do you plan on tying me up to a tree then leaving me for the critters?"

Laughing, I choke out, "No, Willa. Well, tying you up, yes, leaving you, no."

"That sounds nice, sir," she purrs as her grin grows larger when she hears my grit my teeth.

I finally see the lanterns hanging from the large oaks, letting me know we are close. Still on Willa's family's property, I figured asking her the most important question should take place where all the problems started. To close this gap of history and begin anew. My brothers and friends were in charge of sitting up. Reaching the opening in the field, I can see they outdid themselves. The whole area around the pond and trees are lit up with lanterns and firefly lights. Natural fireflies adorn the space as the sky turns to dusk.

Taking deep breaths, I walk to her passenger door, and upon opening it, I take one more look at her before offering my hand. Willa wears a strapless blue dress that matches her eyes perfectly. My fiery angel that I am willing to give my heart and soul to. She apparently always possessed them anyhow. Guiding her out of the truck, I reach back to undo her blindfold. She is breathless, taking in the site in front of her.

Bending down on one knee, I await for her to take notice. Once she does, her hand flies over mouth, and "Hades," flies out of it.

"Willa, my sweet Cherry. My soulmate. We seemed to have strayed off the paths that led to each other for some time. Now that we are on the same path, I choose to only continue down it with you, regardless of what other roads you may lead us down. Love undermines my feelings for you. Everything I feel for you. The intimacy between us is an uncontrolled fire that will never burn out. My endearment to your crass language but refusing to take the lord's name in vain astonishes me daily." She giggles, making my heart clench more. "Your obsession with old westerns and Greek mythology is uncanny, but keeps me entertained. You have re-wired my heart to beat as your own. Your body is the siren that calls to mine. That calls me home. The body that I will worship forever. The lips I will give my last breath too. I will always protect you, respect you, let you fly off the handle for good reasons, punish you when they are not." I waggle my brows and give her a wink. "Support you in all rodeo endeavors. Allow you to truly focus on that if you ever want to leave teaching. I will give you the world, and in return, all I want is you by my side through eternity. Loving me, to be my partner in all things." Opening the ring box, it flashes a simple flawless oval diamond surrounded by tiny ice blue diamonds that sparkle and shine in any light. Just like her eyes.

"YES!" she screams then tackles me to the ground. Straddling me, I place the ring on her finger, then she tackles me in kisses.

Grunting, I mutter, "Willa, as much as I want to devour you at this moment, the gentleman in me feels he must wine and dine you first."

"Such a gentleman, sir." Standing up, I slightly lift her dress and smack her ass, only to find she is completely bare underneath. I lift her over my shoulders, sitting her on my truck's tailgate. Knowing she has a wicked smirk on her face, I try to ignore her, while laying out the blanket on the grass and gathering the basket of food and wine. Once I have laid out, Willa comes to sit on the blanket with me. The stars are now scattered across the night sky giving the perfect backdrop to the lantern lit trees. Sounds of crickets and frogs in the background serenade us as we sip the muscadine wine.

"Nash, this is more than I could have imagined. You are more than I ever thought I deserved. You are right. The word love just does not convey what we have." Now laying with her head in my lap, looking up at me. I slowly glide my hand towards her wetness when she lets the slightest moan escape her lips. My control to ravage her is dwindling. Looking back down to her, she whispers, "more," and that is all I need. Crawling down between her legs, my hands hook her thighs, pulling her closer to me. She pulls her dress over her head, leaving her body naked and open. Just for me. I begin to lick and play with my now fiance.

Pushing my hand down on her lower abdomen, I murmur in a gravily tone, "You taste so fucking good, Willa. Never enough." Plunging my tongue into her pink wetness. Nipping at her folds as her hands grip the earth beneath her. Clinging to this assault of pleasure. My name rolling off her lips in desire, lights more of a bright burning arousal within me. "Let go, Cherry, I have you," I growl out, pushing two of fingers inside to heighten the high. Curling them in against her contacting muscles, causing her to release onto my mouth and hand.

"Fuck," she says in a shortned breath as I continue to lap her cum up, then pushing my fingers back inside of her sleek wetness because this night is far from over. Willa sits up, moving closer to me as my fingers thread her.

"I want more. More you, inside me now." Moving my hand herself, she undoes the buttons of pants, pulling them down with my boxers until my cock springs free. Still pushing down my pants, her head reaches lower until her tongue licks my tip. My beast is unleashed, flipping her over onto her back. I lower myself back between her legs and begin to push into her. Taking her nipple into my mouth, she arches perfectly for me off the ground. Pushing deeper in, against the resistance of her tightness. No matter how many times my cock has been inside her, she is always so damn tight. I fucking love it, I crave the tightness when she is wrapped around me.

"You feel so good. Fucking good." A few strides slowly in and out, her cum coats my dick.

"Nash...please," she begs.

"Be a good girl, Willa, patience." I see the flicker in her eyes before her hips move when her hands grip my ass, slamming me deep inside her.

"Willa," I grit through me teeth. She wants more, I am going to give her more. Beginning to pound hard into her with my hands on her hips, I lift her up to me as I sit back on my knees, giving her all I have.

"More!" she yells. I am driving into her cunt so hard I lose all my senses except the feeling of her tightness around me. I bite into her soft neck, holding back the obscenities I want to shout. She claws at my back like a rabiness animal, knowing she on the verge of her awakening.

"Not yet Willa, not yet." Tears form at the corner of her eyes from the pleasure and pain her body is experiencing. Unwrapping her legs from around me, pushing her knees apart and closer to her body, I continue to slam into her sweetness harder.

"Nash...begging...I..I can't." Moving my hand down to play with her clit and ring, I pull her nipple into my mouth again to suck and bite it, doing everything I know to do to send her in a tailspin over the edge. I am growing closer to the edge as she reaches up and licks my chest, using me as her grasp on life. I'm there with every muscle contraction, and my cock releases deep inside of her. As if her body knows, she clenches harder around me.

"Good girl, milk me as you release over me....... Jesus, Willa." We ride out this tsunami of an orgasm together. My dick is still pulsing inside because I never want to leave her cave. Her falling back on the blanket trying to catch her breath, makes me admire her in a different light. She took a hundred percent of me and never wavered. Only begged for more. My lips trail kisses down her collarbone. "You are one with my soul and body, Willa," I whisper into her ear.

I allow her to roll me over, letting her velvet heat straddle my lap. Reaching behind herself, she gradually massages my balls while rubbing her heat gently against me. Taking no time for my dick to spring back to life and wanting more. She lifts herself then slides down my length. "Let me ride you, Cowboy."
No protests coming from me and pushing her down further, I feel the tip of my shaft hit the back of her insides. She moans loudly, setting off the action of her rotating her hips around me. "Fuck," I drag out as nothing has ever felt this extraordinary, this intense. My hands rise to her breasts to palm, to distract me from jetting in her already.

"Ride me, baby. Ride me." And she does. Quick and hard. Deep and unrelenting, pushing herself into another release, screaming my name into the lit up sky. Before she comes completely back down, I flip her off and set up behind her. Dragging my length down her crack until it finds her opening. Slamming back into her from behind, she arches back, allowing me to wrap her hair around my hand, pulling her back. I don't relent or release her hair, no matter how much she moans and yelps. Because I know she is loving it. She enjoys this roughness I give her. She strives to be a good girl. "Good girl," I say, taking my other hand to slap her ass. She yelps, but she pushes her ass back into me futher.

"More," she moans out so I slap her ass again, feeling her clench around my cock. "You ass and cunt are loving this? Aren't they?" Slapping her ass one more time, because I am coming inside her again, while she rides out another high against me. I pull out while I am still streaming just to let it stream down her ass crack and down her front. Fingering her to calm down her release. "This, this, Willa, is all mine."

"Always," she whispers back. Rolling her over, I collapse half on her and half on the ground to not crush her. Squeezing her into my arms, I tenderly kiss her forehead. This is what I came back for. She is why I survived, she needs me in all the ways I need her.

A year later......

This weekend is everything I have been working for. Ringo and I made it to the American with full sponsorship. Every event we became more of a duo then before. Not that any of it has been unchallenging. I fought with Nash to enter the April qualifying event, but he should have known I would win and prevail. Not just with him but in the event. Including every event after also. Now I am ranked second in the US. If this is to be the final outcome I would be happy. Legit happy. Ringo and I have come so far this past year. Through all the wreckage I have realized how tough I truly am and can drive through anything. Especially with Nash by my side.

I got my girls' rodeo team to nationals, and they brought home the National Title. Now it looks like we are heading back in a few weeks. Though Nash said I could quit teaching, I am not ready to give it up. I am too independent not to have my own income, own job. I know he would hundred times support me and give me everything material because he does this anyway, but the path I forged for myself a long time ago allowed me to be me, and I love all of me, even the broken parts. I need to be busy, use my brain, my hands, and give back. Teaching and coaching allow me to do that daily.

Tilly seems to be less happy with her career, so I find her more often asking if she can cover my lessons and ranch duties. Which has been a lifesaver given how crazy this past year has been. Sometimes I think her and Dirks are the ones running the ranch together, and they always seem like they are up to something when I catch them around. Amity and Blake are still together. I swear they fight over the stupidest shit, just so they can make up. Lana got married back in fall, and of course it was beautiful and all she had dreamt of since being a little girl. She really found Prince Charming, and they are already expecting their first baby this summer. The girls and I are excited to become Aunties and be part of this precious baby's life.

For me, Brooks found himself behind bars for a very extended timeline that not even his dear ol ' daddy can rescue him. Blake ha*s also let me know of his "people" he knows on the inside that will make sure he is well taken care of.* I never ask how he has people, but I have also learned over time, the Holdings have their clutches too. They don't play dirty, but they definitely don't get taken advantage of either. If I have that to my advantage then I am at peace. That asshole deserves every bit of cruel karma coming his way.

Already saddled in on Ringo, we walk up to the release gate. We are up in two. Waiting, I take in the packed arena, the flashing lights, and then my biggest fan, Nash. My now husband. We both had been so busy with all things, that I just handed off the planning to our moms. They have become rapid best friends, and our families are always together when Nash's mom and dad are in town.

When Nash's grandmother first met me she thought I was Ellie. Which I did not mind because she talked sweetly about Nash and I being together and how cute we looked at our young age. It was a sweet glimpse into how their relationship was and what her feelings were about Nash and I. The second time I met her, she recognized me as Willa. Saying how much I looked like Ellie and shared with me their past, shenanigans they used to get into and conversations they had between letters. Along with how Rosa was the bind that twined everyone back together. Never letting up because she saw how much my grandmother and Lainey missed each other. I was ecstatic to be able to honor our families relationship in the wedding with the combining of sands for all of us to have.

The wedding was as lavish and as Texas as one could have imagined. Texas's most sexy bachelor of the Holdings name was officially going off the market, and everyone wanted in. It was a fairytale wedding from riding in on Doc Holiday to the aisle for my pa to walk me, to the I do's, through the reception and night ended in pure ecstasy. Part of my vows to Nash were, he better buckle up because it is going to be a wild ride. So I only laugh to myself when I take a closer look at his shirt saying "Ready for my wild ride" with a vinyl seat belt across the shirt. Shaking my head, I send him a wink, clicking Ringo to move up.

"You ready for this, boy?" I whisper lovingly, rubbing his neck down. He stomps his hoof, giving me the indication he is more than ready. The gate opens as the other rider comes out, and Ringo lines up. Once the buzzer sounds, we take off like lighting.

The End

Acknowledgements

The credit for this story should go to Lainey Wilson. The first time I heard the song "Heart Like a Truck," long before it even hit the radio, Nash and Willa consumed my mind. Willa had a story I needed to unfold and share and I am loving that this story is my first novella. Thank you Lainey Wilson for being a brilliant songwriter and artist. I highly recommended listening to ALL her songs as they are beautifully unmatched and her voice is of a songbird. So many people to give love too! First, thank you to my editor on this book, Jenni Gauntt. Your enthusiastic investment if these characters as their story unfolded filled my heart. Thank you for giving them all the deserved love and attention.

To my PA, Brandi Reyna for always keeping me in line, supportive words and for all the time you put into promoting and editing my books. Along with all the extras she does on the side.

To my TikTok girl, Olivia Matthews. For taking on this app that overwhelms me in every sense when it comes to reels and promoting. For being a wonderful soul that I am thankful to know.

Thank you to all my readers and friends who have supported me through this journey. Including my small town that includes my favorite bookstore, The Dragon's Lair Bookshop, owned by the most beautiful soul I have met, Shauna Cochran.

Thank you to all from the depths of my heart,
Ali Marie

If you enjoyed Heart Like a Truck, (even if not), I would appreciate it if you left an honest review.

Follow Me for more!

Facebook: Author Ali Marie

Instagram: Alimarie_writelife

TikTok: Author Ali Marie

Books by Ali Marie

Bluebonnet Days

Caught In a Storm - book one of the Storm Series

CPSIA information can be obtained
at www.ICGtesting.com
Printed in the USA
JSHW050914161222
34972JS00004B/35